Xanthe of the Amazons. Fate of the Gods

LucaShane Granger

Other Works By This Author

The Silver Fox: Back in the Hunt

Copyright 2014
LucaShane Granger
Cover art by
Jacques Louis David

Dedications

To Homer, for inspiring the setting.

To Thomas Bulfinch, for inspiring an affinity for it.

CHAPTER 1
DELPHI, Ancient Greece

The cave was much cooler than the craggy valley outside. And much darker. Were it not for the shimmering glow outlining the cavern's opening, none would have been the wiser that Helios had already begun his daily trek across the sky.

Of the two figures waiting before the shrine's alter, only one commented upon their surroundings.

"I like this not," he said. "There is something unnatural about Apollo's sanctuary being cast in shadow..."

Rather than basking in the purifying light of day, the sanctuary was hidden away below ground, in a darkness that seemed to defy the whole rationale of that deity to which it was dedicated.

"It is small wonder that this temple is underground," the other said. "It was the Earth Mother Gaia's long before it passed into the care of Zeus and his kin. Another example of the gods profiting off of the work of others."

The one who had first spoke looked about nervously.

"It is not wise to speak of the gods in such a way, Master."

"Your man speaks the truth," an otherworldly voice rang out from the darkness.

Before their diminished sight formed the image of an old woman. Though burdened with the age of many a season, her form remained erect, her countenance proud and unbowed by the passage of time. Her flowing hair shone silver in the dim flickering of the candle light.

"It is not wise to belittle the gods, especially in those places they hold holy."

The one who had done so bowed low. "Forgive me. I intended no offense."

"Indeed," the prophetess replied knowingly. "Is not your whole purpose here an offense?"

The man's servant visibly blanched, but he himself was unaffected.

"Was it an offense when my father heard of *his* destiny? Or his father before him?"

"You speak of destiny, yet I wonder…" her voice trailed off. "At any rate, you are aware of your designs, as are the gods. It shall suffice."

"I would have it no other way," the man retorted, a trace of bitterness seeping into his voice.

"It is a dangerous game you play," the Oracle continued. "You seek to tamper with mechanisms beyond the kin of mere Man."

"Then it is good that I be no 'mere' man." He smiled thinly. "Will you tell what it is I seek to know?"

"You shall know what I know, wither you seek it or no, Zeno of Larissa."

Zeno stood, his arms crossed, waiting. Beside him, his servant looked on anxiously.

The Oracle of Delphi was known far and wide for her prophetic declarations. It was said that the cave's special relationship to the gods imbued its priestess with the uncanny power of Second Sight.

Kings and peasants alike came from all over to know their future. The fate of entire wars had been decided by the auguring that had been foretold therein.

The Oracle closed her eyes, and began to mumble under her breath a tuneless song, her lips tracing syllables that dated back to before the founding of Greece itself.

Zeno's servant cringed as a deep mist, seemingly drawn from the inner bowels of the cave itself, began to form about the old woman, obscuring her already shadowy figure.

"The seat of the Virgin Queen holds the key,

The lock it opens, in the forge across the sea.

There you shall find the tool you seek, fit for a god—and thee."

"Riddles," the servant whispered.

"But with reason," Zeno replied. "I thank you—"

However, the prophetess was not finished.

"Your plan is known to the gods, of that you can be sure," she continued on, in a trance-like state. "They will not stand idly by. Though they are forbidden to act on their own behalf by he whom you despise, mortal surrogates they can draft.

"Beware she who shines like the sun;

Beware also the redheaded one.

Beware he who is Prince of Fools;

And he who is hated by she who rules."

The woman blinked, coming out of her state of reverie. And as she did so, the ominous vapors that had enveloped her thinned and then disappeared entirely, leaving her visible once more in the cave's low light.

Zeno frowned, even as his servant gave voice to his misgivings.

"The gods know what is intended, my master. Surely now—"

"It was to be expected. So, they shall seek to thwart my plans with mortal accomplices… We shall see whom the Fates favor."

Zeno turned to go, gathering his robes.

"Come, Trepat," he said to his servant. And to the priestess, "Oracle, you shall be amply rewarded when my quest is at its end."

"Keep your riches, oh Prince. I think that you shall have need of them."

Curiously, he looked back over his shoulder.

"For payment to Charon for passage."

Zeno's booming laugh lingered long after he left.

CHAPTER 2

"I do not question your judgment, oh Queen."

"Do you not, dear Xanthe?" asked the Queen, bemusement bringing a smile to the usually grim face. "Your very asking of your suitability for the task at hand betrays a lack of confidence in my faculties. Think you that I am enfeebled of mind far before my time?"

"Nay, oh Queen. I sought to—"

"Am I a fishmonger's wife, bereft of sense?"

"Of course not, oh Queen. I—"

"Perhaps you do hold me in the same esteem as one of goddess Aphrodite's worshipers? A love sick maiden whose mind is filled with naught but thoughts of well muscled men and pretty verse?"

"Not I, Queen. I—"

"That is good," the monarch carried on. "For it would be displeasing to think that my own ambassador harbored misgivings of her Queen."

Those assembled in the marble hall fought to keep their composure. Though Amazon warriors the lot of them, they were not immune to the effects of humor. And to the onlookers, the current sight was humorous indeed.

There, seated on her throne upon a raised dais, sat Hippolyta, reigning Queen of this particular Amazon tribe. As in the world of Man, so too were the tribes of Woman separated and spread across great distances, each with their own ruler.

Well formed of mind and limb, Hippolyta seemed as though carved from ivory by the hands of Pygmalion himself. Her hair as black as a raven's wing; her eyes the color of the very Aegean. Even in repose she wore a magnificent armored breastplate with greaves and bracelets, all topped off with a single silver diadem resting upon her noble brow. Every cubit a warrior queen.

And before her, on bended knee, faithful Xanthe.

While no less a warrior than her Amazonian sisters, and no less powerfully built, she nevertheless stood out, even amongst her own kind. Whereas most sported hair the same color as their queen, and some few the color of a newborn fawn, she alone held a head of hair as golden as King Midas' treasure troves. Long and flowing, it cascaded down her back like a golden mane, more suited to a lion than a Greek. It was in fact the source of her name. Xanthe meant 'yellow' in Greek.

But just now that yellow head was bent forward, its eyes downcast.

"My Majesty," she implored, "this is a mission which requires certain... skills, which other of my sisters possess in greater quantities than myself."

Hippolyta's smile widened.

"Very politic, sister. You feel yourself unequal to the task set before you, yet in your own protestations you have shown your worth. My judgment in you is not misplaced."

"Diplomacy has never been a skill of mine, oh Queen," Xanthe said, frustrated.

Hippolyta looked on, amused. "A good warrior knows that the aim of War is Peace. Though father Ares may think differently…

"In that vein," she continued, "if Peace is the objective of War, then it is all important to keep the Peace when it is achieved. Would you not agree, Xanthe?"

"Your logic is unimpeachable, oh Queen. Yet, should not the most steady of us be the one to labor towards that end? For indeed, is not Peace fragile, needing delicate handling?"

The court stood in amazement as their queen went so far as to laugh.

"Oh, dear Xanthe. Always you have felt wanting. Were you not fit for this task, I would not have assigned it to you. Though we have sought to shut ourselves away from the outside world, we are still a part of it. The actions of others may affect our own selves, thus is it the way of things. This you must learn. A warrior must be able to parry with words as well as with a sword.

"That is why you have been tasked with sending tidings of greetings to King Erichthonius of Athens. With the old king we had an alliance. He would leave our lands in peace, and in return we would pledge ourselves to aid him in times of war. Since the throne has passed, we must know if the agreement still holds. If so, good. If not…" she trailed off darkly, all assembled knowing what a 'not' would indicate: War.

"It will lay upon your shoulders, Xanthe, to see to it that the treaty holds."

"I am no wordsmith, oh Queen. How shall I, one untutored in the arts of diplomacy, make a man, any man, heed a course that may conflict with his own base desires?"

"You do pre-judge, Xanthe. Men may see reason when there is reason to be seen. Above all, self interest rules the hearts of Man."

"Why me, oh Queen?" Xanthe burst out.

Hippolyta turned serious.

"I recognize in you that which is marked for destiny. Ever since you were found as a babe in swaddling clothes deep within our forest, seemingly abandoned, I have known that the Fates have a path in store for you.

"Who is to know, perhaps this is the start of that path. Perhaps not. Be that as it may, it can only help you along in that development."

She arose from her throne and stepped down the dais. Tilting Xanthe's head, the queen looked into the troubled blue eyes.

"Oh, Xanthe. You are a favorite of mine. Is that reason enough? See it as the whim of an eccentric monarch." She smiled once again. "You shall excel in this as you have in all else."

"I seek only to not disgrace you, oh Queen. Or my fellow sisters."

"You could never do that, were you to even try."

She bid Xanthe to rise.

"Go now, you have arrangements to make."

Bowing one final time, Xanthe strode out from the hall, her head held high, her back erect.

She was an Amazon, and as such, Hippolyta knew that she would do her duty. For all her words, it was a simple enough task, and there was no reason to believe that the new king would be anything other than happy to renew the alliance. After all, a new kingship was an unstable time. Who knew if old enemies would seek to repay past slights, or if old friends felt the same bonds of affection as before? An offer of alliance should be most appreciated.

It was Xanthe's reluctance to be ambassador that had elevated the situation. If anything, Xanthe could be *too* Amazonian. She wanted nothing more than to fight or to train to fight. Unless it dealt with either blade or shield, she would have nothing to do with it.

There were times when Hippolyta thought that Xanthe would make a better daughter to the war god Ares than herself. Then again, perhaps she was; after all, none knew her parentage, she had simply been found by a patrol. Alone, helpless. And her blond hair *was* rare for a Greek. Mayhap a sign of divine birth?

As far as the Queen was concerned, it did not matter. Xanthe could be the spawn of the lowliest prostitute, and it would not change the affection she held amongst her sisters. Sisters of the sword, if not blood.

It would be good for her to learn that diplomacy was but another arena within which to compete. Words, rather than weapons. Wars could be won or lost just as easily with both.

***

"I admit that I do not understand the Queen's mind in this matter," Xanthe confided, seeing to her steed's halter. She was at the stables, preparing for her journey. Helping her was her fellow sister, Amporna.

"Is it not enough to follow orders? It is a great honor that you have had bestowed," Amporna said, adjusting the blanket on the animal's back.

"This I do not dispute, sister; honor it is. But I am ill suited to this task. It requires a talent for persuasion and sophistication."

"You can be persuasive," her friend answered cheekily. "Do you not remember when Salmantite spread gossip about me? You 'persuaded' her to stop."

Though she tried not to, Xanthe could not help but crack a smile at the memory. Salmantite had lost three teeth that day.

"Crude violence," the blond said, her smile fading. "I have not the skills for well wishing and treaty making. Peacesephtis or Iamgood would have been better choices than I."

"Yet, it is you that our Queen chose."

"It is a puzzle, and I not one for riddles…"

"Then I hope you meet with no Sphinxes along the way," Amporna joked, leaning against a wall.

Xanthe sighed.

"All I desire is the wind at my back, and a sword in my hand."

"What we desire, and what we are destined for are not always the same."

Xanthe snorted. "Destiny. Are you now a seer, Amporna?"

"Nay, yet one needs only to look upon you to know that you are destined for great deeds."

Sourly, Xanthe went back to her preparations, allowing the conversation to drop.

CHAPTER 3

It was a fine, warm, day. The sun shone merrily, its light casting a cheery glow on the forested trail.

Though ill pleased with her current task, Xanthe could not help but feel her spirits lift.

While hesitant about her orders, she was determined to see them through. One way or another she would get the treaty signed. If only she could keep her temper in check…

In scrutinizing the trail for possible sites of ambush, (an Amazon was always on guard) the warrior became aware of voices up ahead. Patting her mount, she urged quiet.

"—you offered to entertain us. What is the matter?"

"Not in *that* manner, 'good sir'."

That was a woman's voice, and she definitely seemed dubious as to the qualities of the person she was addressing.

"Do you think yourself better than us?" another asked. "Our gold is as shiny as any others."

"Of that there can be no doubt, worthy sir." It was the woman again. "However, those be not the wares of which I sell. My stock and trade is of a more literate fashion. Of romance I can tell you. Tales of high adventure I can relate. Even the lineages of the most noble families stretching back to—"

"What we want are deeds, not words, rhapsode," the first one said. "What is that you hide away under yon cloak and robe? A face such as yours puts

Aphrodite herself to shame. You should not conceal that which goes with it…"

Xanthe could hear the laughter of several men. And she could also foresee where this situation was going.

Sliding down from her horse, she unsheathed her sword. Broad at the middle and tapering to a pointed end, it was of typical Greek construction. In fact, she had forged it herself as per Amazon tradition. It was an extension of her own arm. The interweaving leaf pattern on the hilt deceptively feminine in nature. But these leaves held a sharp thorn.

Silently, the Amazonian crept through the underbrush, careful not to make the least sound. Amazons excelled at woodcraft.

Dropping to her stomach, she crawled to the edge of a small rise. She could hear them clearly now that she was practically on top of them.

"I would not recommend this course of action…" the rhapsode said, backing away. "Travelers are under the protection of great Zeus."

"Zeus himself has been known to partake of earthly pleasures. Why should we, mere mortals, deny ourselves?" His leer was explicit.

Xanthe peered over the earthen ledge.

There were five of them. Sturdily built men. From the looks of their clothing, laborers of some sort. At their waists hung various tools, not a proper weapon amongst them.

Five seemingly strong, determined, men who looked to be used to the rough and tumble versus two women, one of which was a rhapsode, a teller of tales, no warrior (even if she did carry the staff of her profession).

It promised to be a massacre.

Too bad for them.

Xanthe smiled, swinging into action.

The group's leader took a step towards the rhapsode—it was as far as he got.

Bursting out of seemingly nowhere, the avenging Fury used the men's disorientation to her advantage.

Lashing out with a blind slash, Xanthe managed to open up the arm of the leader. Howling in both pain and confusion, he withdrew from the fray, nursing his wound.

Even as his compatriots fumbled for their erstwhile utensils, the Amazon smashed one in the face with all the force her fist could muster. The man's nose blossomed with crimson, its owner clutching at it futilely. And before he could do anything, another punch landed to the side of his head, precipitating his slide into unconsciousness, and Morpheus' domain.

Two down in as many seconds. She was getting slow.

Wheeling, the woman warrior faced the remaining thugs. They had their mallets and hammers out, eying her tentatively.

She grinned.

"Boo!"

The men broke like waves upon the shore, fleeing into the woods, dropping their 'weapons' in their haste.

Self satisfied, Xanthe put up her sword. She was about to speak when she was beat to it.

"Stay yourself, warrior."

Turning around, she saw that the speaker was the leader, the one she had cut. Though bleeding profusely, he nevertheless had the rhapsode by the throat with one hand, and a small paring knife held to it with the other.

Strangely, the woman seemed unfazed.

"Pray tell, how do you see this ending?" Xanthe inquired.

The man looked about wildly. His friends had either run off or been left in no shape to help.

"After all," Xanthe said idly, "if all you wanted was to flee, you could have done that before. Now however…" She spread her hands wide.

"Stay back!" He pressed the knife firmer against the woman's flesh.

Then everything exploded.

In a blur of motion, the rhapsode stamped down hard on the man's foot. In pain, he lowered the knife. Then, like lightning, the woman grabbed the arm and flipped him over.

Hitting the ground, he lost both his wind and his knife.

Xanthe stood looking on, impressed.

"A lone woman must be careful in the wide world," the rhapsode said simply.

Grabbing her staff, she gave it a few customary twirls. It was not often that she got the chance to show off.

"Had I not been as surprised by your arrival as they, I never would have been caught unawares."

"I do not doubt it," Xanthe said in all seriousness. "How is it that one such as you has learned the art of combat?"

"As you say, it is an art. Who better to learn an art than a humble rhapsode?"

"Come now," the blond persisted, "How does a singer of songs acquire such a skill set?"

"Very well," the cloaked figure said, good-naturedly. "I do suppose that I owe you for saving me the effort of having to deal with these 'gentlemen'."

Sitting down on a nearby rock, the rhapsode let down her hood, in so doing shaking free a mass of auburn curls.

Xanthe was surprised anew. If yellow hair was rare, red was even more so.

And now that the other had let down her hood, Xanthe could see that she was barely more than a girl, some few seasons younger than even herself. Her face held the unlined promise of youth.

"I am called Glauce, and it was through our sisters that I learned much of the art of war."

"Our sisters?"

"I am what you obviously are: an Amazon. Formerly of Queen Penthesilea's tribe."

Of course, it all made sense now. But she wore the garb of a wordsmith, what could lead to such a thing?

"I can see that you are yet confused," Glauce noted, smiling. "Doubtless you are wondering how a flower of Athena comes to be a rhapsode by profession?"

The blonde nodded.

"It is not a long tale. While my sisters drew from quivers, I did prefer quills. While they coveted swords, I longed for song. It was the stringing of the bow for them, whist I desired the harp. In short, I wished for more.

"As you know, such skills as I sought are not highly prized amongst our sisterhood. So, I took to the open road. A song in my heart, and a staff in my hand."

Xanthe was not sure what to think. Part of her was taken aback by the idea of leaving her fellow Amazons. And yet, part of her admired the girl because it took true courage to set out and do what others say cannot be done, which was the Amazonian way.

"How are you called?" Glauce asked. "I would know the name of she who would be my rescuer."

"Xanthe," she answered, shaking off her lingering thoughts. "Of Queen Hippolyta's tribe."

"Pray tell, Xanthe-of-Queen-Hippolyta's-tribe, what brings you here, on the path of the larger world?"

"I bear tidings of alliance to the new king of Athens."

Glauce brightened up.

"Really? I too tread the path to that throne. The king's coronation is set for two days hence. It will be a time of much merry making. A rhapsode will be in great demand.

"As will your gesture of continued friendship, no doubt," she added. "Would it not make sense for us to travel together? There is strength in numbers, and it is not often that I am fortunate enough to partake of the company of one of my fellow sisters."

It sounded good to Xanthe, and she said so.

"Good." Glauce paused. "What of this lot?" She nodded at the groaning, bleeding, figures at their feet.

Xanthe grinned.

"They wished to see what you looked like under your clothing, let us see how *they* measure up."

"I do believe that this is the start of a most fortuitous friendship."

Before long, four people were on their way. In one direction two as carefree as a jaybird; the other, two as nude as one.

CHAPTER 4

Athens was amidst a time of rejoicing. The streets throughout the city were clogged with revelers. It was a time of renewal, rebirth. A new king had assumed the throne, always a time of hope.

Some hoped for continued prosperity. Some for newfound opportunities. Some for the retrieving of lost ones. Whatever their desire, they came to the city from leagues around.

Xanthe looked about, unable to disguise her wonderment. Everywhere she cast her gaze there were people laughing, haggling, talking. A sense of frenzy hung over the city like a physical presence.

Vendors hawked their wares. One was selling dishes already embossed with the image of the new king. Another offered commemorative sculptures. All loudly attested to their quality and craftsmanship.

"Never have I seen its like," Xanthe said, still twisting her head this way and that.

"You need to see more of the world, sister," her companion told her. "There are many sights and sounds beyond those of the din of battle. The residents have a new king, and look forward to what it may herald." She paused, peering at something. "And it would seem that they are not alone." Pointing, the rhapsode indicated an enclave of finely dressed men. From their attire, as foreign as the Amazons themselves.

"Others come bearing glad tidings to the new king. From Troy, I should say."

"You know this how?" Xanthe asked.

"Their manner of dress. It is of the fashion of Troy as of late. A rhapsode must keep abreast of such goings on."

"I brought no finery with which to greet the king," Xanthe fretted.

"Fear not," Glauce reassured. "As an Amazon, you shall not be expected to present yourself bedecked in the garbs of royalty. Ours is a reputation for being quite Spartan in dress."

Finding a place to stable her horse, Xanthe and Glauce made their way through the throngs to the palace.

"I would have a word with the royal chancellor," Glauce explained. "Oft times they are most knowledgeable of their denizens, knowing the best places for a rhapsode to make her daily bread and the like."

With no small effort, the duo eventually found themselves at the steps of the palace. It was all that the guards could do to keep the citizenry in check. They spared no time for the two Amazons.

"It is the excitement," Glauce explained. "Everyone from the lowest beggar to the richest merchant seeks an audience with the king."

"I must get through, even if I must make myself a way," unconsciously, Xanthe gripped the hilt of her blade.

Glauce sought a different tack.

"Come," she touched her sword sister on the shoulder, "There be more than a single method to dressing a lion."

Leading the way, the rhapsode moved within the sea of humanity until she spied a side alley. Signaling Xanthe to follow, they made their way down the space between buildings.

Far from being dark and dank, the passage was fairly lit by the sun overhead, and due to its proximity to the city's royal residence, free of the trash and debris that was to usually be found in such places.

"How are your climbing skills?" Glauce grinned.

The space between the buildings that formed the alley was large enough to walk through comfortably, but narrow enough that were a person (or an Amazon) to stretch themselves out lengthwise, they could touch both structures—and crabwalk their way up.

In a trifling, the two managed to crawl/climb their way to the rooftops. Amazons were raised to climb nearly as soon as they learned to walk.

Using the rooftops as a path, they were soon standing across the way from the palace. Glauce pointed to a spot on that building's high wall.

It was a window, with a balcony around it.

"We are to jump?" Xanthe wanted to know. The distance between them and the window was no mean one.

Glauce nodded.

"Then I hope you are not out of practice, sister." Smiling, Xanthe backed up to get some room. Setting her stance, she erupted in a frenzy of motion.

Legs pumping, arms churning, she reached the edge of the rooftop and threw herself out into space.

It seemed as though time stood still as the Amazon hung out there in the void. It was oddly quiet, only the rush of her own blood sounding in her ears.

Then with a whirl of activity, the spell was broken, and she landed on the balustrade, having cleared the balcony's rail.

Looking back, she saw Glauce prepare for her attempt.

Her short stature had always hampered her in events that required reach. And the fact that she was wearing a hooded cloak did not help matters any.

Throwing her staff across to Xanthe, Glauce took a breath, the Amazon-turned-rhapsode calming herself. Letting the breath out, she started out slowly, gaining speed as she neared the lip of the roof until finally she leaped, arms outstretched as far as she could.

Even as she flew across the intervening space she began to lose altitude.

Her face etched with concern, Xanthe watched as her newfound friend appeared to be shorting it.

At the very last instant, Glauce's fingers managed to curl themselves around the railing, even as the rest of her body slammed into the side of the building.

Grabbing her friend's arm, Xanthe hauled Glauce up onto the balcony. Slightly out of breath, she got to her feet.

"Would that I possessed Hermes' winged sandals…"

"It was close."

"Close only counts in farm implements and Greek Fire."

Taking their leave, the two entered into the palace proper. Fortunately for them, the room was unoccupied. Obviously a bedchamber, they quickly made their way to the hallway adjacent. At both ends were staircases. One leading up, the other down.

"Which way?"

"Down," Glauce said, giving the matter some thought. "The throne room would be at the ground floor, so as to hold audience over public matters."

Taking the spiraled staircase down, it was not long before they came to another landing. But before they continued on, they were met with a challenge.

"Who goes there?"

Turning, the duo saw what had to be a palace guard. Though he seemed ill suited for the task to the warriors' jaundiced eyes.

While tall, he was thin as well. All gangly limbs and awkward features. Xanthe privately wondered if he could withstand a stiff breeze without falling over.

And instead of the typical palace livery, his armor was a conglomeration of competing and contrasting styles and makes. Greaves from Sparta. Corinthian breastplate. Trojan gauntlets. Even a helmet of Illian design. He resembled nothing if not a purveyor of junk.

"Is that a soup pot he wears upon his brow?" Glauce whispered to her friend.

"I said, 'who goes there?' " the man repeated. "It is customary to answer, lest I be forced to take you prisoner."

The Amazons smiled.

"I am Xanthe, representative of Queen Hippolyta of the Amazons. I bear greetings to the new king. This," she nodded to her side, "is Glauce, a rhapsode by trade. We seek the throne room."

"The throne room? That is on the main floor. How is it that you have found your way up here?" He eyed the pair suspiciously.

"We took a shorter route," Xanthe deadpanned.

The guard looked about to inquire further when Glauce intervened.

"What is your name?"

"I am known as Iochier." He stood up to his full height, thrusting his chest out.

"Iochier," the rhapsode wheedled, "could you be of service to two lost women who seek only to bask in the glow of your lord's gracious presence?" She went so far as to bat her eyelashes.

It had the desired effect.

"I suppose that is not unreasonable… After all, the royal palace is no place for two women unescorted. Even if you are armed…" His gaze fell to their weapons.

Leading the way, Iochier descended a flight of stairs. And another. And then up one. Up, down, down again. This continued for an unspecified amount of time.

"Iochier," Glauce called out, "do you know the way to the throne room?"

"I *am* a palace guard, am I not?" he replied evasively.

"How long have you been a palace guard?"

"Since this morning."

"Since this morning…"

"After all," he equivocated, "I am a warrior, not an architect."

"Are we to understand that we are lost?" Glauce asked, incredulously.

"This way," Xanthe said. Having had enough, she took a staircase at random.

As Glauce made to follow, Iochier spoke up, hesitantly.

"Hold! I can not allow two armed strangers to wander about the palace unescorted."

"Then 'escort' us." The blond battler pinned him with a look that could cut glass.

Clearing his throat, Iochier hurriedly got in front of the duo and proceeded to lead the way down the staircase Xanthe had picked out.

***

Thus far they had seen no one, yet while passing through yet another corridor, a din came to the trio's ears.

As they got closer, the sounds became more distinct.

"What is it?" Iochier asked, noticing the women coming to a stop.

"Those are the sounds of battle…" Xanthe remarked. "Come!" With that she sprinted down the hall towards the noise, Glauce at her heels.

Befuddled, Iochier stood still for a moment before he took after them. "Wait!"

The ring of bronze on bronze sang out a siren's call that inflamed the Amazon's blood.

Standing before her was a set of ornate double doors, gilded in gold and silver. They served notice that they stood sentinel over something of great value. But now they merely hung splayed out against the wall, a silent testament that they had failed in their appointed task.

Through the now open doorway, Xanthe could see the source of the conflict.

Inside, battle raged between the palace guards and several unidentified men, who for their part were trying to make their leave with something. What, she could not tell. But it was enough for her that they were thieves.

Unlimbering her sword, Xanthe let loose the war cry of her people, plunging headfirst into the melee, with Glauce soon following as Iochier struggled to extricate his own blade.

With a wild gleam in her eye, and a snarl on her lips, Xanthe cut a swath through the would be robbers, aiming a vicious cut at the head of one of their number.

Taken by surprise, the man barely managed to get his own sword up in time to block.

Shooting a knee, the Amazon caught him in the groin. Pained, he doubled over, which opened him up to the hilt of Xanthe's sword, which she brought down on his unprotected head. Immediately, he collapsed like a wet toga.

Turning around, she was met by another brigand. Thrusting, he tried to skewer her like a piece of mutton.

Twisting aside, she dodged the attempt while cleaving at the man with her own blade. Arcing through the space separating them, its momentum was barely slowed when it impacted with the man's neck.

Awash with the geyser of blood that followed, Xanthe presented a formidable figure to all who saw her.

Not far away, Glauce was holding her own.

Using her staff, she managed to trip up one bandit from behind. While down, she hit him on the head to make sure that he stayed that way.

Making a feint towards another attacker, she thrust at his partner, catching him in the 'bread basket', knocking the air out of him.

Ducking, she avoided the swipe the other took at her, and in so doing brought her staff up, striking him on the chin. His head flying back, he was unconscious before he even hit the floor.

Meanwhile, Iochier's scabbard was proving stubborn, as it failed to heed his repeated yanking. So focused was he on the task, that he failed to take notice of his surroundings. And it was this inaction that spared him a quick death.

Catching a thief's wrist, Xanthe head butted the rogue, bringing stars to both of their eyes. But the Amazon was too far gone in the blood wrath to care. She smiled at the pain. It was good; it fueled her rage, an asset in pitched battle.

Her opponent dropping away, Xanthe saw *him*.

A man in his thirties. Average height. Typical dark hair. But it was his bearing, and his clothing, that made him stand out from the others. He was not just a thief; it was obvious that he was the leader of this merry band of cutthroats.

While his men fought, he made busy taking a small chest down from a pedestal. It was only then that Xanthe noticed that the room in which they all stood was in fact a temple. Above the pedestal stood a frieze of Hephaestus, the Metalsmith of the Gods.

***

When Zeno had finally figured out the first part of the prophecy, he had been daunted. That was until he remembered Athens, and its seat of power: the royal palace. And to that end he bribed a member of the palace staff to reveal any 'unique features' of the place. So when he was informed that a small temple dedicated to Hephaestus was set deep in its depths, well, he was sure that was where he would find what he sought.

Infiltrating the palace had not been hard—people were coming and going at all times due to the festivities. And with the information provided by his spy, they had been able to find the temple with ease.

It had been bad luck that some of the royal guard should have happened by as he had entered. But that did not matter, for he had gotten what he had came for.

Taking a small wooden box down from a pedestal, Zeno gazed upon his prize when a blur of movement caught his eye. Turning, he saw her for the first time.

A woman. A warrior. A warrior woman with a wild blond mane, the luster of which rivaled that of the noonday sun… It was as if a cold hand had reached into his chest and plucked at his heart. For the first time, fear of failure crept over him.

The priestess had told him to beware the one which shone like the sun.

"Trepat, come," he ordered, a note of anxiety in his voice. "Let us away from here." With that, he hefted the box, trusting its contents to no one.

***

Xanthe saw the man making a break for it. But even as she gave chase, she was set upon.

Quickly blocking the killer's blade with her own, she spun around and bisected the attacker from behind.

Dripping gore, the warrior woman looked back only to see that it was too late—the leader had gone.

She took out her frustration on those remaining. A whirling dervish of death, none could take their eyes off of her.

Soon an entire troop of palace guards arrived, with none other than their new king at their head.

Silently, he surveyed the damage done to the temple. Before him were the bruised and battered remains of both guards and foemen alike.

Of the latter, only one had been left alive. Bleeding, and clutching a broken arm, he cowered under the glare of the new king of Athens.

"I am Xanthe, ambassador from Queen Hippolyta of the Amazons," the Amazon spoke, gaining the king's attention. "She bears you greetings."

"And I bear *you* greetings, Xanthe of the Amazons. It would seem that today is a day for strangers in our midst."

"They did happen upon us as we were repelling the brigands attack, Your Highness," one of the guards said.

"The attack…" The king now looked hard at the limp figure being upheld between two of his own bodyguards. "What did they—" he cut himself off mid-sentence as he saw the grand pedestal empty, the box which had sat atop it now gone.

"The key…"

Whipping around, he grabbed the lone remaining thief by the front of his tunic.

"Who hired you? Where is it?"

"If I may…" Xanthe offered, bowing low.

Nodding, the king stepped aside.

Staring down, the Amazon affixed her unflinching gaze on the rogue.

At first the man tried meeting it, his eyes defiant. But before long, doubt began to creep in. Soon he felt the need to look away, but could not bring himself to do so.

He began to sweat, unable to find any solace from the unrelenting view. Time seemed to stand still as Xanthe's glare filled up the very universe itself.

"Make it stop! Make it stop!" he pleaded, struggling to pull himself free.

"Answers!"

"I know not what or where the object of which ye speak be. I swear!" He was on the verge of tears. "The man never said his name, he paid us to help him loot your palace."

"Fool," the king remarked. "Know you not the penalty for such a transgression?"

"We were promised rewards, fabulous treasures that we deemed worth the risk."

The king brought his face close. "Does it appear so now?" Disgusted, he turned away. "Take him to the dungeons, I shall attend to him later."

"And what of he who escaped, Your Majesty?" one of the guards asked.

"I want every available man—"

The young monarch was interrupted by a deep thrum that pervaded the air, causing the temple to fairly shake, such was the intensity.

A look of grave concern came over his face. Hurriedly, he began to hustle everyone out.

"Out, out. Quickly."

Bewildered, Xanthe and Glauce hung back as the soldiers were shepherded out, save for Iochier, who had been slower than the others.

The king turned to them, even as he sought in vain to shut the ruined doors.

"You must leave, forthwith. You can not—"

Again the king was interrupted, but this time it was by a voice.

"Hold, Erichthonius, King of Athens. They too must hear what I hath to say."

Unearthly, the voice seemed to emanate from everywhere and nowhere at the same time. An incredible volume beyond that of mortal means. Deceptively calm, as the sea before the storm. Strong. Vibrant. Feminine.

Even as these impressions were made, the air before them began to glow, and then slowly thicken into a solid mass.

At first vague, then by degrees more and more defined, until finally it assumed the guise of a woman. Then, in a final burst of light, she was revealed, full born.

The draped robes. The high, crested helm. The unnaturally bright shield in one hand, the shining spear in the other. None could mistake her.

Athena, beloved daughter of All Father Zeus, Goddess of Wisdom, the patron deity of both the Amazons and the city of Athens.

The king and the Amazons immediately bent to one knee, with Iochier following suit.

"I bid you welcome… Mother."

Glauce's eyes widened at the appellation, as did Xanthe's. Mother? Yet Athena was known far and wide as a virgin goddess.

The goddess-made-flesh smiled. A warm, mirthful smile, as though she had read the Amazons' confusion from their own minds.

"As a babe, Erichthonius was given unto mine care, and I in turn entrusted him to the good people of Athens. A people whom I hath nurtured as though they wert mine own offspring."

"I am honored as always by your presence," the king said, reverently.

"Would that it were under more auspicious circumstances," Athena's voice echoed with a cosmic weariness.

"Oh Mother, is the removal of the key your will?"

"Nay," Her eyes flashed like ice upon a bright winter's day. "It is the will of another. One who would seek to make himself a god."

The king stood, befuddled.

"I do not understand."

Athena looked about the battle-scarred temple.

"Thou shalt."

Walking (gliding?) to the ruined doorway, she waved a hand, and suddenly there stood the doors, whole, and good as new.

"He whom hath stolen the key doth be known as Zeno. He would hath it for his own dark purposes."

The goddess continued to amble slowly about the temple, restoring it to its former unblemished state.

"I shall have the entirety of the guard turned out. The whole city will be scoured until we find him." the king vowed.

Athena held up a palm. "Already he doth be beyond thy walls. Even now he speeds away, bent upon his ends." Her eyes clouded, as though seeing events that transpired far away.

"Great Athena," Xanthe beseeched, surprising herself, and drawing anew the goddess' attention. "You did speak of divine aspirations. Pray tell, whom does this Zeno be, and how does this 'key' aid him in this quest of his? That is, if it is thy will to reveal such information to the likes of us." she finished, remembering to whom she spoke.

The Goddess of Wisdom's features softened, alighting on one of her beloved Amazons.

"Ah, Xanthe. Always to the heart of the matter. Hippolyta did well in her choice of ambassador. Would that all held such clear convictions as thyself…" Shaking her head, she let out a godly sigh.

"However," she continued, "all do not. Such it is with Zeno. The key which he hath stolen doth be of no ordinary contrivance, nay, but rather an artifact created by none other than Hephaestus himself, forge smith of the gods."

That would explain its presence in one of his temples, but why *this* one? And if it was a key, what did it unlock?

"It unlocks a hidden door to Hephaestus' forge on Mount Etna, in Sicily, across the sea," the goddess answered the unspoken question. "With it one can gain access to the god's earthly domain—and with that, access to his works."

"That a mortal man should gain entry to the domicile of a god…" Glauce breathed softly.

"Not mortal," Athena corrected, "but half-mortal. Or, more accurately, a demigod. His mother was a mortal woman, but his father is the same as mine own… Great Zeus himself." The admission seemed to leave a bad taste in the goddess' mouth.

"I confess, great Athena, that I do not understand." Glauce blanched at addressing one of the gods.

"Glauce," Athena said fondly, "always questioning, always seeking to know. Xanthe knows, is that not so?" She turned towards the Amazon warrior.

"I believe so," she said slowly. "It is an ancient story—power. You did say that this Zeno is a demigod, yet it is not enough. He seeks to become a full god. Hephaestus must possess something to help him achieve this end, why else seek a way into his sanctum."

Athena beamed.

"Thou art indeed a credit to thy gender. Thy mind is as sharp as thy blade."

"Yet I remain puzzled," the golden haired Amazon confessed. "Of all of Hephaestus' temples, why was the key to his godly residence kept here, in the first house, of the first city, of *your* heart?"

"I can answer that," young Erichthonius said. "My father did wish for me alone to have access to him whenever I desired, thus he forged the key for such visits."

"Your father—"

"Is Hephaestus," he finished.

Xanthe and Glauce looked at him with new eyes.

"When I was born, he realized that a forge was no place for an infant babe—even one whom was half-god. Thus he turned to his sister Athena, who in turn saw to my upbringing amongst the people of Athens."

"Who in turn saw fit to make thee their king." Pride shone in the goddess' voice. "Of thy own account thou hast risen high amongst men. A credit to mortal and immortal alike."

"Key or no key," Glauce pressed on, too full of curiosity to feel properly awed, "Hephaestus would surely know that someone was in his abode, unwanted or no."

"Wert he there, yes. But even he must leave for Olympus when summoned, thus even now his lair lays fallow."

"What forging of the gods can convey godhood upon men?" Glauce wanted to know. "As a rhapsode, I have heard that there are but three ways for one to gain the ranks of the immortals. Direct bestowment from the gods themselves—"

"Which shan't happen." Athena stated flatly.

"—through digestion of Ambrosa—"

"Which may only be procured from Mount Olympus itself."

"Or through the acquiring of a golden apple from the Grove of Hera."

Athena looked at her anew.

"Thou hast learned thy lessons well. In truth, Zeno seeks entry to Hera's sacred grove. Though in order to accomplish that, first he must attain the proper armaments. Thus comes Hephaestus' part to play. Zeno seeks to steal nothing less than father Zeus' own mighty Thunderbolts."

The very idea of it sent a shudder down their collective spines.

"Wert that alone the extent of his ambitions it would be crime enough…"

"What else could he wish?" Glauce was aghast. "What is there to aspire to beyond becoming one of the gods?"

"To rule them."

Those assembled stood motionless, mute testimony to the enormity of what she had said.

"Zeno would use his newly acquired immortality to assault Hades' very domain in order to free the Titans from their long imprisonment and forge an alliance with them to overthrow the gods of Mount Olympus—thus making himself King of the Gods."

The Titans. The rulers of the cosmos before the coming of Zeus and his kin. In point of fact, Zeus' rise to power was due to a great cosmic war between his cohorts and the old guard, the leader of whom had been his own father, Cronus.

At the end of the day, Zeus and his forces had been victorious. The Titans had been tossed into the depths of Tartarus, never to be freed. Only a handful had been spared the Olympians' wrath. And no doubt those who did had no desire to see their own number return—as 'traitors' they were sure not to be well received.

That a man, even a demigod, would seek to usurp the cosmic order. It was beyond belief. Had anyone else spoke of it, it would not have been given credence. But that it came from the lips of Athena…

"It is this point in the drama that thy own part is to be played. *All* of thee…"

Following the goddess' gaze, they all turned to see Iochier—who had been in the midst of slinking away from the temple unnoticed.

Flashing a weak smile, he came to attention.

"Zeno's mad plan must not be allowed to come to pass. Against this blasphemy thou shalt serve as the divine retribution of the gods."

"Uh," Iochier blushed as once again eyes sought him out. "If his plan be known to the gods, why is it that you do not strike him down yourselves? Turn him into a tree or some such..." his voice faltered as the Olympian's fathomless eyes bore into him.

Suddenly, the goddess sighed.

"Thou knowest not how I—and my brethren—would dearly love to do so. However, father Zeus is extraordinarily fond of his children, especially his sons." She sighed again. "He refuses to take the situation seriously, he doth believe that Zeno will not go through with his scheme. As such, he hath forbidden us from harming the upstart. Thus, we art forced to act through proxies."

"Us?"

"Thou."

"To what do we owe such distinction?" Xanthe again. "Why is it that amongst all the children of the earth we are the ones you have given this task?"

"Fate is a thing that even the gods art powerless before. Thy actions in this matter were foreordained, beyond the reckoning of both mortal and immortal alike."

"That the fate of gods should lay in the hands of mortals..." Xanthe could not even finish the thought, such was its enormity.

"What do you require of us, oh Mother?" Erichthonius asked, unhesitantly.

"Thy role hath been fulfilled, Erichthonius of Athens. No more can be asked of thee, save that thou aid these others on their way, for their journey will be long, and fraught with peril. And success doth not be assured, even with the favor of the gods."

Another smile tugged at the Goddess of Wisdom's lips. "And I would recommend that thou doth accept Queen Hippolyta's offer of alliance."

"It shall be so," he agreed immediately. "I shall send an emissary to her tribe forthwith."

"No need." Athena said. "I shalt convey the tidings myself, as well as explain to good Hippolyta that she shalt be bereft of one of her sisters for the foreseeable future."

Spreading her arms wide, the temple was once again bathed in a golden light.

"Fare thee well, mine champions," she bade, her voice echoing from the walls. "Know that the gods travel with thee in spirit, if not in flesh."

And with one last blinding flash, she was gone.

In the afterglow, those assembled looked from one to the other, the import of the situation laid fully upon them.

"Truly, a better start to a tale could not have been crafted, even were I the one crafting it." Glauce said, shaking her red locks from side to side.

CHAPTER 5

Everything had happened so fast. *Too* fast for Iochier, still somewhat amazed at finding himself on a horse and on his way.

"Madness," he muttered, "sheer madness. This is a task fit for the gods, not mortals."

"You heard Athena as well as any," Xanthe replied, not bothering to turn in her saddle. "Zeus has forbidden the gods' interference, thus it is left to us."

"Three lone mortals, two of them *women*," he paused at the look Glauce leveled his way. "Er—*Amazon*s," he corrected, "are to travel into the unknown—"

"Not unknown." Xanthe corrected. "We do know where Zeno goes. It is our task to track him down before he achieves his aims."

"Yet, already he has a start upon us," Iochier pointed out.

"The lead be trifling. We shall catch him."

Iochier did not share the golden haired warrior's confidence.

"Pray tell, what is to be done then? Are we to take him to Mount Olympus bound in chains?"

"He raises a point," Glauce agreed. "Goddess Athena did not direct us as to how to stop Zeno. If Zeus has bade the gods to not harm his son, how cross might he be at us lesser mortals for doing so?"

For the first time, the golden haired beauty turned to eye her companions.

"Come what may, when the time comes, what needs be done shall be done."

Even if one were to argue with her words, none would have been so inclined to argue with her eyes. As cold as the frozen north, they conveyed unmistakable resolve. She would see this through—to the ends of the world if need be.

***

Leaving the city center behind, they raced for the docks, the very lifeblood of Athens. The sounds of commerce mingled with the smell of the salt air as Xanthe inquired as to the recent activities of the port.

From the oldest grizzled fisherman to the youngest galley mates, none could recollect having seen a ship, any ship, having left the harbor within the past day, let alone the past hour. Rather, the place was filling with those *arriving* to witness the coronation of the new king.

"I confess to being at a loss," Iochier said, lifting his bowl like helm to scratch his head.

"Somehow I suspect that to be the natural order of things with this one…" Glauce confided to her Amazon sister in an undertone.

"It would appear that Zeno begins to show his craft," Xanthe reasoned. "Knowing that the open sea be the most obvious route, he opted to not take to the water."

"Which means—"

"That he did choose to evade us with a trek over land."

Glauce screwed up her face. "Difficult indeed will it be to find the trail of a single man leaving a city the size of fair Athens. All the more so with the celebration bringing people in from far and wide."

"You have answered your own query," Xanthe pointed out. "People are coming *into* Athens by the droves. Those *leaving* are conspicuous indeed."

"A man fleeing while others arrive? Such should make an impression indeed."

The truth of that belief was borne out fairly quickly. A survey of the merchants who had camped out in the city confirmed that a person matching Zeno's description had been seen leaving in great haste on horseback.

An added piece of information was that another man followed. Most likely a servant.

Most importantly, a direction was given: Northwest.

Reigning her horse around, the blond beauty gave vent to an Amazonian hunting cry and set out at a dead run.

Echoing her friend's shout, Glauce kicked her own mount into action.

Iochier's beast, caught up in the excitement, followed, leaving its rider hanging on for dear life.

CHAPTER 6

"My lord," Trepat ventured, even while the mare's hooves beneath him attempted to drown out his voice, "where are we heading?"

"Megara," his liege replied, looking back. "From there we can depart for the open sea."

"Surely they will follow."

It was something that had preoccupied Zeno's mind. If only there were a way to delay his pursuers, or better yet, take them out of the equation entirely… That he had seen the one who 'shines like the sun' could not be more plain. As such, it was fair to assume that the others mentioned in the prophesy should be with her, and all after *him.*

It was those engrossing thoughts that prevented him from realizing the change in his horse's stride until suddenly it came to a skidding halt, nearly sending Zeno flying head over heels.

Getting his bearings, he heard, as well as saw, what it was that had frightened his mount.

Cackling evilly as they sailed on the winds, their long hair fanned out about them, were a covey of the scourge of the skies: Harpies. At least a dozen of them.

Horrendous creatures, they were half woman-half bird. The face and torso were those of the fairest of women, marred only by a cruel beauty, concealing both a ravenous hunger for human flesh and rows of sharpened teeth.

Gnarled and clawed, the Harpies' feet resembled nothing if not a bird of prey, ready to render and tear those poor unfortunates that suffered to get too close. And from their backs sprang wings. Wings larger than that of any fowl.

"What hath we here, sisters?" the obvious leader cooed, her voice belying the fair visage of her face.

"Man-flesh," another answered, her tongue caressing the filed points that served as teeth.

That the situation was grim, Zeno recognized immediately. Fast action was called for if he did not want to end up the Harpies' next meal.

"Hold, good women." He nearly choked on the 'good'.

The Harpies laughed.

" 'Good Women' art we?" one asked, amused. "Pray tell sisters, doth we be 'good'?"

"No!" was the chorus.

"Sisters, doth we even be 'women'?"

Again, "No!"

"It would appear that thou art wrong on both accounts, Man-thing." She grinned wickedly, her teeth on full display. "More is the pity—for thee."

This was not going well.

"Again, I say hold!" he demanded imperiously. "You would devour the Son of Zeus?"

Though they did not back off, Zeno could tell that he had given the Harpies pause.

"Thou doth claim divinity?"

"Through my veins flow the blood of Olympus."

Shocking him with her speed, the lead Harpy flew up to Zeno, grabbed him by the front of his tunic, and smelled him. Deeply.

A look of disgust crossed her face.

"This one reeks of the gods," she said, before subjecting a terrified Trepat to the same process. "But this one…"

"Is my manservant," Zeno finished.

Shooting him a look, the Harpy let go of Trepat and rejoined her sisters.

"What be thy business, little godling?"

"My activities are mine alone to know," he replied, thrusting out his chin.

"Zeus has so many children," one of the brood piped up, "surely he will not miss one…"

"Why settle for us when you could have Amazon?"

At the mention of Amazons, the Harpies flew into a frenzy—as he had hoped. It was well known that Harpies held a deep-seated hatred of the women warriors. The Amazons sought to live in the world of Man rather than put it to the torch. To the Harpies, this refusal in allying themselves in a great struggle to crush humanity was tantamount to betrayal of their gender.

"Speak, godling."

Zeno cleared his throat. "Even now one follows behind. A fine specimen, fit for your stew pot."

"Why should we not merely eat thee and thine in *addition* to this other of which ye speak?"

"Good will. Is your lot in life so fine as to turn away divine benediction? My father, Zeus, would not forget a kindness shown to his son on your part..."

"To hath the gods be in our debt would be of interest..." one proffered.

The Harpies were silent as they contemplated the potential benefits. Only the continual flapping of their wings could be heard as a gentle breeze wafted over those assembled.

Finally, the one who had first challenged the wayfarers spoke.

"Tell us more of this Amazon..."

***

Unlike their prey, Xanthe, Glauce, and Iochier were slowed by virtue of following.

Though they had surmised his direction, he could be headed anywhere along that line, thus they had to take the time to find Zeno's tracks, and even more time following them.

It was while following this trail that they came upon an inn set up along the roadside for those weary travelers who wished a bit of bread and a bed.

"It is nearly nightfall," Glauce remarked. "We shan't be able to track Zeno in the dark. Would it not be prudent for us to seek shelter until the morn?"

Though reluctant to give up the chase, Xanthe was forced to agree with her logic.

"You are right," she admitted. "As soon as we come to a suitable—"

"I believe that we already have," the rhapsode pointed out, indicating the inn. "While as adept at sleeping out in the open as any of our breed, I confess to preferring a soft bed to the hard ground."

"I cast my lot for the inn as well," Iochier made known.

Xanthe stared hard at him, then the coming twilight.

"So be it."

Leading the horses to the stables out back, the trio soon made their way into the inn proper.

The door opened upon a large common room, already filling up from those farmers and merchants who had finished business for the day.

Stares followed them as they approached the long bar.

"What can I get you?" the innkeeper asked, wiping his meaty hands on a greasy apron.

"Lodging," Glauce replied.

"Amazons!" one of the patrons shouted. "As clear as the nose on your face, they be a couple of man haters! Unnatural, women bearing weapons. Mikos, since when have you allowed the likes of them into your establishment? They want wine, I say let them pick some grapes; that's the place for women." Laughing, the man drained his cup.

Mikos, the innkeeper, looked at them apologetically. Xanthe, though irked, was willing to let the outburst pass; she had bigger fish to fry. But Glauce was not so sanguine.

"If our 'place' is the cultivating of fields, are we to assume that yours is the sowing of them?"

"I could plow your field, little girl." The smarmy remark drew some laughter.

Glauce pretended to reflect.

"I can see that," she said. "You *do* bear a striking resemblance to an ass…"

The man's face darkened as the crowd roared at his expense. Drawing himself up with a great show, he made to confront the rhapsode.

Xanthe had had enough. "Sit down."

"Why? Who are you to command? Do you pretend to royalty? Ho, ho!" he addressed his fellows. "We had better pay deference to her majesty here. I beg your forgiveness, oh mighty Amazonian Queen!"

"I be no queen."

"Eh, what is that, Your Highness?"

"I said that I be no queen." Her voice held an edge to it now.

The man sensed a sore spot, and pressed home.

"Come, show us your scepter of state! What regal raiments does a Queen of the Amazons wear?"

The blonde's jaw worked as she sought to not lose her temper. Even now her hand itched at the hilt of her blade…

"What was that, Your Highness?" the man jibed, "I do not think that we heard you?"

"She said that she be no Queen, man!" a voice boomed. Like the growl of a bear amongst the bleating of sheep, it was distinctive.

Looking around, Glauce saw a wall of patrons part, revealing the speaker seated at a table in the far corner. She was left agape.

If the man had sounded like a bear, he more than looked the part as well. Even while sitting, it was clear that were he to stand he would tower head and shoulders above all others in the establishment.

And such shoulders! His musculature was as well defined as if it had been chiseled from marble, a specimen whose proportions conjured up thoughts of mighty heroes of myth and legend.

Arms and legs the thickness of tree trunks, and equally knotty, bespeaking great strength. Hands that looked as though they could strangle an ox.

And across the great frame was coarse black hair, coming into its own in a thick full beard. Even the hair on his head struggled against the leather band holding it out of his eyes.

And yet his clothing was as outsized as the man himself. Rather than a toga, or a robe, he wore instead an animal skin carved from a single beast, like some savage from a foreign shore. The pelt was that of a mighty lion, and as it encircled his breast and loins, its fully intact head formed a hood that the man might utilize to ward off the elements.

And there, resting at his knee, was an enormous war club, worn smooth as if from much use. And next to it, along with a quiver of arrows, laid an equally massive bow, which doubtless its owner alone could bend.

The physique, the attire, the armaments. There could be but one man who strode the earth as such, one *demigod…*

"Heracles," the redhead whispered.

"Cease your prattle, man. It is enough to sour one's wine. Mikos," the living legend turned to the innkeeper, "drinks for the house, on me." He smiled at the resultant cheer that went up from the crowd.

Chastised, the drunkard slunk away, even as Heracles got to his feet.

" 'Amazon Queen'." He chuckled. "I have known Amazon Queens in my travels. Pray tell good warrior," he addressed Xanthe, "are you familiar with a queen of your people by the name of Hippolyta? Quite a woman, that one." He smiled, the pearly white luminance of his teeth stark against the dark backdrop of his bearded face.

Xanthe glared at him, coldly.

"Indeed. She is my liege."

Heracles laughed, a hand coming down hard on the bar in amusement, causing it to shake.

"It is a wonderment to be sure, the actions of the Fates. Do you know *me*?"

"All the world knows of you, Heracles, Son of Zeus. Loved by the King of the Gods, hated by their Queen. Aye, all know your name, but we Amazons know it best of all. It was you that stole the enchanted girdle given by Ares himself to my own Queen Hippolyta!" Now the ice in her eyes was replaced by fire.

"We did offer you hospitality, and you repaid us with treachery and deceit! Aye, you are known to us, and we spit at thee!" And matching action to words, she did just that.

The room went deathly quiet. Glauce was stunned, and the innkeeper ducked underneath the bar, only to find Iochier already there.

All were on pins and needles, waiting to see what would happen next. Xanthe stood her ground, unflinching in her treatment of he who was renowned as the greatest hero in an age of heroes.

Heracles' reaction surprised them all: he laughed.

A magnificent laugh, a laugh that seemed to fill the room even as it shook the rafters with its vigor. At it, Xanthe's expression turned to one of puzzlement.

"Forgive me," the Son of Zeus said, his frame still quivering in merriment, "I laugh not at your harsh judgment of me, but rather at the irony of it. You would see me dead for what is to you a crime, and in truth, one was mayhap committed, yet not the one you think."

Heracles could see the confusion written large upon Xanthe's face.

"Come, sit with me and I shall tell you a tale…"

Warily, yet undeniably intrigued, Xanthe followed the demigod back to his table. Her companions followed suit, Glauce giving Iochier a strange look as he emerged from his hiding place.

"I suppose that it can do no harm now. Long years it has been. In truth fair Amazon, I never stole that girdle from your Queen, and indeed, it is questionable if I could, had I tried. Hippolyta is a feisty one." The corners of his eyes crinkled in a smile.

"It was of your queen's own free will that she gave me her magical girdle."

"Why would she part with such a divine gift? The pride of our tribe?" Xanthe asked, unbelievingly. "Especially to a man."

"A token of affection."

"Affection?"

"She parted with her girdle to aid the completion of my Labors." At that, a haunted faraway look came into the demigod's eyes.

The blond battler's head spun.

"Had your tribe known the truth, Hippolyta would have been killed. Thus I suggested that I be made out a villain, that I did take advantage of her good graces and stole the item instead. I had the girdle, and she did get to keep her life and position."

Had her tribe thought that its queen had given away its most prized possession of divine making, to a *man* no less, she would have been executed. It would have been seen as a betrayal to the sisterhood.

"What is your opinion?" Heracles asked straight out. "Is your Queen a cheat to her people?"

Xanthe did not know what to think. If true, *should* she be held as guilty of a crime against her sisters? The revelation shook her, yet a lifetime of memories were unchanged. Her queen had done a great deal of good for the tribe during her tenure on the throne, and doubtless was a great leader.

Glauce could see her newfound friend's dilemma, and sought to alleviate it the best that she knew how.

"Hippolyta's girdle was a gift given to *her* by her own father, Ares. A gift to *her*, not her people. As such, it was her own personal property to do with as she pleased. And if it pleased her to give it away…"

What it meant to be an Amazon had been put to the question. She had been taught since childhood that men were inherently bad. At best a necessary evil, if only to produce more women.

But to think that Hippolyta, the very essence of Amazonian ideals, had not only formed an attachment to one… Not just that, but had seen fit to give, *give*, away the most scared relic of her people to one—with naught in return, knowing full well the condemnation her people would heap upon her…

And then she had seen fit to allow the lie of her actions to lay with her sisters. An Amazon was to never lie to another—the code of the sisterhood.

All of her training, all that she had been taught, was it all empty words? How could one be Queen of the Amazons and yet abandon their ways? Did that make Hippolyta unfit for the tribe? Or was it the tribe that was unfit for her?

In point of fact, it was true; the girdle was hers and not the tribes'. Also true was it that Hippolyta had never actually claimed that Heracles had stolen it—it had been assumed as such. Was omission of the truth itself a lie?

But if Hippolyta was to be found blameless, then did that not mean that the Amazons sensibilities themselves were at the root of contention?

"Listen to your friend," Heracles bade, "she has right of it. Your queen is no less regal for what she has done. It was an honest gift, given honestly."

Heracles turned to Glauce. "Pray tell little one, what is so important as to bring such a disparate pairing together as the three of you?" Lifting a beaker, he drained it in one motion.

"We are on a mission for the gods." Iochier responded, unthinking.

Glauce elbowed him in the ribs, sending his own drink down the front of his mismatched attire.

Heracles laughed again.

"So, the gods," he mused, stroking his beard. "What mischief are they up to now?"

"You speak such of the gods?" Iochier asked, his tone low, his head swiveling from side to side as if he expected one of their divine order to show up at any second.

"Forget not that I am partly of their race. Who better to know their ways than I?" Wiping a hand across his mouth, he went on. "They inspire no reverence in my heart for I know them to not be my betters. In truth, few of them do I even consider my equal!"

"Please, Heracles," the barkeeper implored, twisting his apron in his hands. "It is dangerous to speak such of the gods."

"Bah. That speaking the truth should mark one for retribution…" Sourly, he took the new mug offered and quaffed it.

"Still," he said afterwards, "they do serve a purpose from time to time. Pray tell, what has my family sent you in search of? A monster to be slain? A relic to be retrieved? A bet to be won?"

"It is nothing less than their own existence!" Iochier revealed, his tone hushed in awe. Had she been within range, Xanthe would have smacked the man. As it was, Glauce did it for her.

"Ow!"

"Indeed." Now the demigod's curiosity was aroused. "It does sound most grave. That Olympus itself should shake… I must know, to what ends has my family directed you?"

Xanthe and Glauce looked at each other. The cat was out of the bag now.

"Are you familiar with one by the name of Zeno?" Xanthe asked, making a decision.

Heracles thought a moment, then shook his head. "Nay, the name means nothing to me."

"His sire be the same as your own: Zeus."

Heracles chuckled. "Father Zeus spreads his seed around; not unlike the trees in the olive groves he so loves! Many are those living whom I can claim kinship to through him. Be they gods, men, or monsters."

"Zeno intends to overthrow your father and all of Olympus and declare himself supreme lord of the heavens and earth."

"A tall order."

"He has a plan," Glauce took over. "The first step of which is to steal Zeus' Thunderbolts for his own use."

That raised the hero's eyebrows.

"Such a plan would mean trespassing upon their maker—"

"Hephaestus, yes, we know. He intends just that, to steal upon the god's abode while he is away."

Heracles rubbed his chin. "Conceivable."

"He then intends to gain immortality by attaining a golden apple from Hera's sacred grove."

"I could almost admire the man." A twinkle was evident in the demigod's eyes.

It was well known the enmity held between Hera and Heracles. In fact, his very name had been a vain attempt at mollifying the Queen of the Gods. To her, he was a constant reminder of her husband Zeus' infidelity. As such, she had bent her will to destroying him.

While still an infant in the cradle, she had sent two snakes to kill him. Yet to everyone's surprise, little Heracles had strangled them. From there she only ratcheted up the assault on the demigod's life. Were she not expressly forbidden by Zeus himself, she would have long ago personally taken her revenge. But Zeus tended to shield his own: a trait that Zeno had come to benefit from.

Glauce plowed on.

"And with immortality, he shall invade the Underworld and free the Titans from their long imprisonment."

At that, the great hero's brow furrowed.

"Such a war would devastate mankind, if not wipe it from the earth like crumbs from a table."

The giant of a man folded his arms and sunk his head, deep in thought. Xanthe was surprised to see this aspect of the man-god. She had thought him a braggart—albeit one who could back up his high opinion of himself. But to see him in contemplation was unexpected.

At length, he unfolded his massive arms, and looked Xanthe in the eye.

"Know that you have the Scion of Olympus' aid in your quest. Verily, my club and bow are with you." He slammed a fist down in determination, forming a large crack down the entire length of the table.

Eying it, Xanthe could not deny that the demigod's strength could be of great use. However, Athena had said nothing about adding to their party. Indeed, she wondered as to the wisdom of telling him this much.

Even as she thought it, she felt a tap on her shoulder. Annoyed, she turned around to see a cloaked figure. A voice issued from within the folds of the garment.

"Accept his offer."

Slipping back the hood, the figure revealed itself to be none other than Athena herself. Astonished, Xanthe looked to her comrades, who, save for Heracles, were equally nonplused.

"Well met, sister," the Son of Zeus greeted the goddess.

A slight smile played at her lips. "Greetings Heracles, thou doth appear well."

"In spite of Hera's best efforts." The hero grinned.

"In truth," Athena added for the benefit of the others, "I doth not share Hera's enmity towards Heracles. How could I? For he doth be mine own half-brother through our father Zeus."

"A fact that will forever mark me down in Hera's bad graces."

"Forever is a long time…" the Goddess of Wisdom said, a far away look in her eye. "There may yet come a time when thou art welcomed to shining Olympus with open arms."

Heracles snorted. "When pigs fly."

Athena's smile broadened. "I shalt see Circe about that."

The goddess then turned to Xanthe. "Their eyes art unseeing," she answered the unasked question.

In truth, Xanthe had wondered at the goddess' open revealing. Yet now, following her gesture, the Amazon could see that none of the patrons had moved. They all stood where they had been, stopped in mid-movement, frozen in space.

"They are as props in a play…" Glauce marveled.

"As good an analogy as any," the goddess conceded. "Dear Xanthe, thou would do well to take Heracles up on his offer, for he too doth hath a role to play in this drama."

"Make no mistake, sister. I bear no great love for the gods. It is not a credit to them that things are best when their actions are least. That the best of the lot are the least active says multitudes. Present company excluded." he added, softening his tone.

"However?"

"However, it is as I have said. This scheme of Zeno's would bring naught but more suffering to Man. Thus, once again, Heracles must come to the aid of the gods."

Straightening up, he seemed to fill the room with his presence.

"Wait."

All eyes turned to Iochier, who, in a sudden moment of insight, had found his voice. But now, with everyone looking on, lost it again.

"Yes?"

To hear the Goddess of Wisdom address him with such equanimity lent him strength.

"You did say that the gods are forbidden from interfering with Zeno, is not Heracles a god?"

Athena smiled, indulgently. "Nay, mine half-brother is only part god; he is also part mortal. That renders him immune to the edict."

Glauce looked at Iochier, impressed. Whether because he managed to think up the question or that he had seen fit to voice it, he could not tell.

"Fare thee well, oh champions. The fates of both mortal and immortal alike depend upon thee."

And in a flash of light she was gone.

"Now that my sister has graced us with her presence, let me tell you of the time I fought the many headed Hydra…"

CHAPTER 7

The weather promised to be clear, free of any unpleasantness. Which was good, for they would need to travel some distance.

Mounting up, Iochier noted that the demigod was without a steed of his own.

"What of Heracles?" he asked.

"I have no need of horse, good Iochier. The Scion of Olympus is fleeter of foot than any steed. Have you ever heard of the time I ran down the Golden Stag…?"

As the Son of Zeus launched into another of his past exploits, Xanthe went over in her mind what needed to be done.

Zeno had had an entire night's worth of travel time on them, and what was more, his tracks would become increasingly difficult to locate as he traversed more and more well trod paths.

"We shall catch him," Glauce said, seemingly reading the mind her newfound friend.

"We must," the blonde said simply. "Failure is not an option."

The rhapsode nodded solemnly.

Giving the signal, Xanthe urged them down the road; all the while Heracles continued with his tale, showing no strain whatsoever, speaking and jogging to the horses' gait.

***

The morning wore on uneventfully. Contrary to her previous misgivings, Xanthe could see that Zeno's trail was clear. Strangely so. This path seemed little traveled. But why?

***

"The godling said that there was but one. I doth spy four."

"True, sister, yet it makes little difference. We be many, whilst they be few."

From their vantage point high in the sky, the harpies gazed hungrily.

"Today we feast on man-flesh!"

***

"The Fates are kind," Iochier emoted.

"They had best be," Heracles said, eying his much slighter comrade. "It is their own necks we aim to save."

"I find your attitude puzzling, Heracles," Glauce ventured, giving voice to her thoughts. "You are a demigod, yet disavow your divine heritage."

Heracles grimaced.

"I know their true nature. They are to Man as Man is to monkeys, and in that lies the question that if Man is above monkeys, and the Gods are above Man, what is above the Gods? After all, did not father Zeus come from Cronus? And did he not in turn come from Uranus? And was he not the heir of Chaos? Where was *he* birthed? The gods self-style themselves the masters of the universe, whilst in reality they are but its children, same as Man. Yet they set themselves apart, and have the temerity to dictate what is and is not. All are subjects to a greater divine will. And it is to this divine animated spirit that I pledge myself, no false would-be 'gods'."

The idea was intriguing to say the least, and it was the sort that set the rhapsode's mind to racing.

"What be those?" Iochier suddenly cried, pointing to the sky.

In the distance could be seen a dozen or so black specks against the blue backdrop of the heavens.

"Birds," Glauce replied, dismissively.

Xanthe's gaze lingered.

"Nay, not birds. See how they become larger as they near."

"*Large* birds?"

"Were they Griffins, the shape would still be wrong."

Soon the specks became more than specks, and their shape lengthened and stretched.

"Harpies," Xanthe and Heracles both realized.

The wild light of battle kindling in his eyes, Heracles grabbed up his war club.

"Already it would seem that my services are needed. It is a pity that there are not more of them."

" 'More', he says." Iochier groaned.

Now it was clear why the trail was so lightly traveled. Obviously this was a place locals knew to avoid.

But the time of avoidance was past. Now was the time for action.

Grabbing up her sword, Xanthe made ready for the aerial invaders, even as the others did the same.

The winged she-beasts gave vent to an ear splitting shriek as they descended en masse.

Shouting in defiance, Heracles and Xanthe's war cries rung out as well.

The Harpies knew the first signs of trouble when Heracles, swinging his war club with a two-handed grip, knocked the head clean off of one of their number; sending it flying through the air like a rocketing meteor.

"This would make a fine sport to add to the Olympics!" the demigod laughed.

Xanthe's horse pranced about nervously, its eyes rolling dangerously. So it was that the Amazon found herself fighting not just Harpies but her own mount as well.

The blonde bobbed to her left, avoiding the first frantic clutchings of the winged monster's sharpened, claw-like fingernails, even as her steed sought to throw her to the ground.

The current situation being untenable, Xanthe made the only decision that she could. Using her momentum, she rolled out of the saddle, freed from encumbrance.

The Harpies made for their hated enemy like darts seeking the bulls-eye. In turn, Xanthe made for them.

A heartbeat from colliding, the Amazon executed a summersault—sailing over the monsters.

It was in mid flip that the warrior struck. Her blade flashing, she sank it to the hilt into the back of one of the harpies.

Holding it fast, she shifted her body around and was soon astride her new 'mount'.

Flapping her wings furiously, the harpy attempted to relieve herself of the unwanted passenger, all the while screaming all manner of obscenities.

So erratic were her actions that her sister was unable to aid her in her hour of need.

Grabbing a handful of hair, Xanthe wrenched her ride's head back, causing its entire body to jerk higher. Using her newfound rein, she 'urged' the fiend forward—straight into the harpy's sibling.

The two knocked into each other in a mass of wings and limbs. Yanking her sword free, the blonde dove free, even as the two monstrosities fell to the earth tangled together.

Horrified, Glauce saw her friend streaking towards the ground. But even as she was about to cry out, Heracles was on the scene, and with a speed belying his large frame, caught the freefalling Amazon in his arms.

"The best thing to have come from the heavens since Prometheus brought fire!"

In a wink the Amazon was back on her feet.

"Move!" she said to Glauce and Iochier, noting their gazes. "There is a battle to be won!"

Starting, the two followed her into the fray.

Swinging her staff, Glauce caught a harpy upside the head. While profoundly strong, harpies could still be hurt by mortal means, as Xanthe had shown.

Meanwhile, Iochier ducked a wicked looking talon. Rolling, he came up in a fighting crouch—facing the wrong way.

"Behind you!" Glauce yelled.

Whipping around, he missed being beheaded by an eyelash. Eyes wide, he thrust out with his sword, piercing the harpy's wing.

Giving forth a cry of pain mingled with anger, she launched herself bodily at the Greek—mouth wide open, fangs at the ready.

Before Iochier could respond, the fiend at his throat was roughly knocked away by one of her own sisters colliding into her. The toothy horrors rolled along the ground, entangled.

"For being able to fly, they do toss worse than an overripe melon."

Turning, Iochier saw the grinning face of Heracles.

While Iochier enjoyed a reprieve, Glauce still struggled with her adversary.

The rhapsode leaned back, avoiding the clawed specter. Then, with reflexes born from a lifetime of training, she jabbed with her staff, catching the monstrosity in the eye.

Howling, the harpy clutched at her wound. And as she did so, Glauce took advantage and plowed the end of her staff into her stomach.

With a *whoosh* of air, the harpy fell to her knees. Like lightning, Glauce brought her staff down hard over the creature's exposed head.

Crack, and the harpy lay still.

For her part, Xanthe connected with a left cross, staggering the longhaired terror that sought her as its next meal.

Grimacing, the Amazon flexed her hand. That would hurt later.

But it had accomplished its objective. Off balance, the harpy was easily toppled as Xanthe followed up with a shoulder tackle.

Then, with a foot on her foe's neck, the Amazon thrust home with her sword, piercing the creature's black heart.

Coldly, she pulled the gore-encased blade free, seeking more prey for its insatiable appetite.

By now the tide of battle had become clear to the pack of would-be man-eaters.

"It was not supposed to be this way, sister!"

Seeing them hesitate, Heracles threw back his head and shouted at them.

"Come, tarts of Tartarus! Have at thee! See if you can do that which even Hera herself has failed at. Test your mettle against the Scion of Olympus, the Son of Zeus. Come, Heracles commands it!"

The harpies halted, clearly unnerved.

"Heracles?" they whispered to each other, hovering far from the demigod's wrath. Or so they thought.

Throwing down his club, Heracles unshouldered his great bow, one so large that but a handful in all the world could string it. Withdrawing an arrow from his quiver, he quickly notched it. Then, taking careful aim, he let the missile fly.

All this was performed in the merest of twinklings. Before the harpies knew what was happening, one of their number dropped silently to the ground below, having taken a bolt through the throat.

That was the breaking point. With a great flapping of wings, the abominations fled in all directions as quickly as their limbs could take them.

A hand before his eyes, Heracles watched them go.

"Pity. They were proving great sport."

" 'Sport' such as that I can do without," Glauce remarked.

Xanthe too watched their enemy depart, but she was silent.

"It is small wonder this path be little trod. With creatures such as those, I should wonder at any man's sanity to travel this route!" Iochier exclaimed, checking himself over for damage.

"Yet Zeno passed," Xanthe finally spoke, breaking her reverie. "He has made it past unmolested. How?"

Heracles had the answer.

"There is always a larger fish. Doubtless, Zeno bespoke of us to the harpies, enticing them to devour *us* rather than himself."

"They nearly succeeded," Glauce groused, adjusting her raiment. Cloaks were not made to fight in.

"Mayhap this is to our advantage," Xanthe mused. "If Zeno thinks us dead, his pace may slacken…"

***

The flapping of leathery wings heralded the harpy's arrival. Pulling on his reins, Zeno stopped his horse just as the apparition landed before him.

"Liar! Cheat!" she screeched, pointing an accusing finger.

Looking as though she had been battling a Cyclops, the bruised and cut harpy presented a most battered image.

"What do you mean?" the would be god replied, trying to recover from his surprise.

"Curse Tyche that our luck should be so bad as to meet with *two* spawns of Zeus!"

"What?"

"Heracles! Had I and mine sisters known…!" the creature wailed.

Heracles? What was *he* doing here? Then he remembered. The prophesy. This changed things dramatically.

While lost in his own thoughts, Zeno failed to notice the change that came over the harpy.

"Thou wert the one who convinced us to attack! 'Twas upon thy recommendation that so many of my sisters now reside in the Halls of Hades! It is only fair that thou goest to join them!"

Howling like a Fury, she raked at the demigod, intent on dismembering him. However, the blow never fell.

Shrieking, she grabbed at her side, staring dumbly at the green ichor that spilled through her fingers.

Trepat looked upon his handiwork, bow drawn again, ready to loose another volley.

Made cognizant to his dilemma, Zeno franticly pulled his sword. Then, without preamble, cut off the harpy's head.

Brains and gore littered the ground where the monster fell.

"My thanks, Trepat."

The servant nodded. "My liege."

"Come, we must away from here, with all speed."

CHAPTER 8

"Megara is a prosperous port," Glauce remarked, turning in the saddle in order to better see.

While not boasting the exoticness of Athens, Megara nevertheless accomplished a cosmopolitan feel. What with being a seaside city, it received all manner of goods and people by way of trade on the Aegean Sea.

Silks from Troy. Wines from Egypt. Rugs from Persia. Even spices from far away Catharay. All combined to fill the city's treasury, which it in turn lavished on its architecture and storefronts. Even the average merchant could afford to standout like a peacock amongst geese.

Yet as the group made its way down the crowded street, checking out the sights and sounds, one of them was notably unimpressed.

"Come now Heracles," Iochier said, smiling in spite of himself, "surely you must admit that this be better than detouring as you wished."

The demigod was silent, his face grave, as though he were not quite focused on the present. "Let us see to a ship and be gone."

Elbowing his way through the crowd, he outdistanced his comrades.

Iochier looked on, puzzled. "What has come over him?"

"Aye," Xanthe nodded thoughtfully. "His spirit flagged when it was decided to book passage here. Why this city should be less palatable than any other…" she let the quandary hang in the air.

"Of course!" Glauce exclaimed, snapping her fingers. "Megara!" she said brightly. Then, a second later, more sedately, "Megara."

"Aye, that be the city we are in." Iochier confirmed, confused.

"No," Glauce explained. "You do not comprehend. Megara is the reason for Heracles' mood."

The two looked at her. Iochier bewildered, Xanthe patient.

"Are you ignorant of the history behind this city's name?" the rhapsode asked.

"My talents do not lay with History," the blond remarked, dryly.

"Heracles, his Twelve Labors. Surely you are familiar with *them*?"

A smile tugged at Xanthe's lips. "Even were I not before, how could I help but be after hearing tell of them from their participant?"

"Do you remember the cause of them?"

The blonde battler furrowed her brow. Glauce took it as leave to continue.

"Hera, Queen of the Gods, wished to cause Heracles great grief, yet was forbidden from harming him directly by Zeus, thus did she set upon the plan to have his wife and children slain in order to cause him to suffer indirectly.

"Using Mania, the Goddess of Insanity, as a proxy, she did command her to invade Heracles' mind, and using him as a vessel, slay his family.

"Though blameless," the redhead went on, her frame all aquiver in the telling of the tale, "he did, does, blame himself for their deaths. As such, he sought redemption by submitting himself to a base king. Thus were the Labors brought about.

"This city," she swept her arms wide, "is named in his wife's honor. The very place reminds fair Heracles of his loss and shame."

"Why did he not speak of this?" Iochier asked.

"Would you?"

"Come," Xanthe said, seeing the object of their discussion getting out of sight. "This only gives more incentive to be away from here as quickly as we may."

***

The dock lay swathed in silence. The fresh moon shone on the water's mirror-like surface, broken up a hundred times as the waves lapped gently against the stone pier. Perhaps in time it would succeed in its age-old struggle against the earthen obstruction, but not tonight. Tonight was to be given over to other struggles.

"If you wish passage, you must pay. Even Charon does not work for free," the swarthy captain laughed.

Trepat looked around the inn, a look of trepidation mingled with disgust. It reeked of stale wine and lost ambition. Would that they could manage the trip alone. But it could not be. And it would take too much time to buy a ship of their own and outfit it. No, they were forced by expediency to throw their lot in with ruffians.

"Master," Trepat bade, his voice low, "are you certain that men such as these are to be trusted?"

"Trust has naught to do with it," Zeno answered. "They possess a fast ship and are willing to take us where we need to go."

"I fear that they shall cut our throats ere long, before we reach our destination."

"I would not put such an action beyond the rogues. However, they would forfeit their whole fare. Half of their payment they receive now, the other half when we are safely landed at Sicily."

"They may feel that one bird in the hand be worth two in the bush."

"Greed, Trepat. Greed. It does rule even the basest of bloodlusts. We be of more worth alive than not. It is simple business."

With that, the demigod returned to the sea rovers, lifting his cup in the air for a toast.

"To fair winds, and even fairer rewards!"

Roaring with approval, the men slapped him heartily on the back.

"That is what I desire!" the captain grinned toothily. "Rewards!"

"You need not fear," Zeno said, filling the man's cup to the brim. "You shall receive all that you deserve…"

***

"I still am of the opinion that we should have been off as soon as possible. I like not the effect this place has upon Heracles." Glauce frowned into her cup.

The room buzzed with activity, night having fallen and the day's careworn labors forgotten. In their place, the city's nightlife came out, eager to help wash the memories away with all manner of libations.

Yet the three sat alone in a corner, apart from the merrymaking of others.

"There is not a single honest ship that would hazard from port at night. Not even a slavers galley," Xanthe replied. She too bore a grim countenance.

"I too dislike the mood that has struck Heracles," Iochier said. "That a name alone should send him into such a fit—"

"I doubt you would be of any merrier disposition were you in his sandals," the redheaded rhapsode scolded. "Is your heart made of stone? Are you truly insensitive to his plight? Have you—"

"Nay, I gainsay him not," Iochier interrupted. "Rather, I was agreeing that I dislike his mood."

"There is agreeing, and then there is *agreeing*..."

The argument drifted away as Xanthe rose and left their table.

Heracles' lassitude was infectious, his demeanor had brought them all down as surely as a right cross to the jaw.

Enjoying the coolness of the evening after a day spent on the trail, Xanthe wandered aimlessly through the city's byways. She marked that even at this late hour the citizenry were out and about. Did this city never sleep?

As she passed by another wine house, she glimpsed through the open doorway to see none other than Heracles himself.

Hunched over, head hung low, he sat alone at a table that seemed ill suited to a man of his frame. Even in silence he dominated the room. A wide space was left between he and the rest of the patrons.

"More wine," the demigod demanded, not bothering to lift his eyes.

Before long a cup was set before him. He grunted thanks.

"Be that how Greeks speak to one another?"

Looking up, he saw his server to be Xanthe. Without asking, she pulled up a bench and sat down.

Gazing about at the assembled customers, she took note of their strenuous efforts to avoid looking towards the two of them.

"Why is it that you are not regaling all and sundry of your tales of past heroics?"

The Scion of Olympus gave a non-committal grunt before taking a long swallow.

His eyes were dark, his lids heavy. His melancholy was palpable.

Xanthe felt that she should say something. But what? Where another might have drawn off of her womanly intuition, she was an Amazon. And Amazons were not known for their empathy.

Thus, Xanthe found herself sitting uncomfortably in silence. The minutes dragged by until she could take it no longer.

"The warrior who fails to bespeak to her defenses can never hope to know victory," she said, awkwardly.

A low rumble emerged from her companion. At first she thought it was a belch. But presently Heracles smiled, showing it to have been a chuckle. Weak, but a chuckle nevertheless.

"You are no Homer. But your point is well taken."

"I shall leave poetry to Glauce. My art is that of War, not words."

The demigod's mournfully downcast eyes failed to leave his drink.

"Oft have I thought how my life would have been altered had I been a playwright telling of the world's stage rather than being a player upon it."

"Poorer, I should think," the blond stated bluntly.

Heracles looked up.

"That the hero of Greece should waste his prowess on ink and parchment," she continued, "it is unthinkable."

"I had thought that your opinion of me was quite low. Naught but a base criminal."

Now it was Xanthe's turn to avert her eyes.

"You have given reason for much thought in our short association. It is a poor general indeed who hangs onto a course of action in the face of new intelligence."

Heracles sighed. "Would that my own opinion of myself were as easily changed." He upended his cup, draining it of its contents.

"Tell of her. What was she like?"

The hero continued to avoid the Amazon's eyes. "Who?"

"She for whom this city is named. What manner of personage was she?"

The demigod seemed to sink within himself, his perpetual good spirits extinguished.

"Were I to say 'sweetness and light', it would be true enough. She had patience beyond passing. Would that her temper had been hotter; she might have spurned my advances, and thus saved herself…"

He toyed idly with his now empty cup. Unsure as to what to do, Xanthe merely sat, waiting.

"She was a princess; by both birth and manner. I did save her father, King Creon. Grateful, in his generosity he saw fit to bestow his daughter's hand in marriage.

"You would be right to scoff at the idea of me and that holy institution," he continued. "As my father before me, I have been known to have sown some wild oats. Unknown are the number of children I may have sired in my lifetime. A mere mortal might spread his seed far. How much more then might a demigod?

"Yet, I would have it known before Aletheia, Goddess of Truth, that I never strayed while Megara lived. She alone captured my attention so wholly.

"Her strength of character matched my own physical traits. Where others would tire of my antics, she stood fast. While other women would flee from the doom that played about me due to Hera's undying hatred, she stood firm."

"A woman who would defy the Queen of the Gods must have been indeed remarkable," Xanthe remarked.

"Aye, she was…" Heracles stared off at some distant point that only he could see. "And suffer greatly for it she did." His voice became hard.

"It was too much for Hera to stand, that I should find happiness. No, that was not to be tolerated…"

"The gods torment us so because they envy us," the bearded muscle man said suddenly, switching gears. "For all their might, they envy Man for his passions. Love. Contentment. Wonderment. Things that they, from their fastness far above, can never know.

"They treat Man as children, yet it is they who are childish. Their intrigues, their affairs, they but seek to mimic Man, as though by doing such they can know what it is to feel human. Bah."

Heracles continued.

"Megara did outshine all other women. Whilst others have leapt into my bed, she did make me pursue her. Though I was to be given her hand, I needed to *win* her heart. As you are aware, the harder the hunt, the more valued the prize."

Xanthe understood.

Heracles sat looking at his hands. As though seeing them for the first time, he would turn them over slowly. One would think they held the answer of the ages.

This was an entirely different side to the demigod, and it continued to challenge Xanthe's views of him, as had all his actions since they had met. He was a contradiction.

To her people he was a criminal. Yet his very actions denied this.

By his own proclamations he was a braggart. Yet his achievements were such that he lived up to his boasts.

He was a demigod amongst men. Yet he disparaged his divine heritage.

He was known as a womanizer, yet he had been a faithful husband.

He was prone to mighty mirth and mighty melancholies.

In the end he was as much a puzzle as the Gordian Knot. The Amazon could do nothing, save sit and provide a sounding board for the broad chested Greek.

"Hera sent forth the mad goddess Mania to do her bidding, to make me an instrument of my own destruction. As a puppet, my actions were controlled, guided. To those whom I had pledged my life and honor did I lay low."

For a long moment he sat silent, words seemingly useless. Yet at length he continued.

"I personally had not been harmed, thus father Zeus' prohibition was seemingly not violated. And what was more, it was not Hera who had acted at all, but Mania. She whom the gods regard as mad, too crazed to know her own complicity. What blame can be attached to a crazy woman? Or for that matter, a crazed god?

"It was a masterful plan on Hera's part. She was free from the vengeance of all. All save myself."

His eyes smoldered as his muscled neck knotted with tension.

"Someday there will come a reckoning between her and I. And Olympus shall shake to its very foundations when it happens."

Xanthe doubted it not. To be forced by the gods to slaughter one's own family… It was a thing that she had a hard time coming to grips with. It was enough to shake one's faith in the gods.

"Though the actions had not been of my own volition, I did perform them. I felt the need for atonement."

"Thus, The Trials," Xanthe concluded.

"Aye, The Trials."

Increasingly unsure of her own mind, Xanthe sat with the Son of Zeus throughout the balance of the night.

***

The morning brought a peerless blue sky, and a sun that blazed merrily, lending its benediction to the activities of the foolish mites that toiled away beneath its singular gaze.

The wharf was humming. Fishmongers already hard at work hawking the day's catch, fishermen mending their nets, slaves being transported to auction, the place was as busy as an anthill.

Amidst this maelstrom stood the four adventurers, ready to start forth on the next leg of their journey.

Heracles, somber, even in the light of the newborn day. Xanthe, showing not an iota of fatigue after having stayed up all night. Glauce, looking forward with anxious anticipation. And Iochier, ill at ease, casting dark looks at their mode of transportation.

"This is it? We are to traverse Poseidon's realm in this?" the latter voiced his concern for the derelict before them.

"She may not be fair of face, but she be limber of limb," the ship's proprietor said proudly. "Not a faster ship will you find."

Xanthe arched an eyebrow.

"Here," he amended. "At this dock. Right now."

Glauce gave the blond battler a sideways glance before addressing the ship's owner.

"I am sure your worthy vessel shall perform to our specifications."

"She has been known to accomplish the Kessel Run in under three parsecs. She shall deliver you to your destination."

The man patted the ship's prow, un-phased as paint flaked off into the harbor.

Single masted, the ship was no more than ten or eleven cubits long. The owner assured them that what it lacked in size (or looks) it more than made up for in speed. And in truth its long lean lines did bespeak of being built to cut through the waves.

"What say you, Heracles?" Xanthe asked, turning to her compatriot. "You have had the most experience in these matters. Be the ship fit?"

"It is small enough that we need no crew other than ourselves. And it does appear to have survived more than one season out at sea.

Though not the *Argos*, it should take us where we need to be. Aye, it will do."

The owner beamed. "Excellent. As to the manner of payment…"

As Xanthe paid the man, Glauce gazed dreamily at the watery expanse.

"The sea."

"The sea," Iochier echoed, with much less enthusiasm.

"The majesty…"

"The churning waves."

"The power…"

"The upset stomach."

"The romance…"

"The sharks."

Glauce sighed. "The sea."

Iochier also gave vent to a sigh, one born more of resignation than appreciation.

"The sea."

CHAPTER 9

Zeno stood at the ship's prow, watching as it cleaved through white tipped waves, racing him towards his destiny. He breathed deeply, savoring the tang in the air.

"Soon, Trepat. Soon."

"As you say," his faithful servant replied from his place behind his master.

"Before us is my rightful place in the cosmos. No more shall I be denied my station, no more a bastard to be ignored, but rather, a god amongst gods."

"The Titans—"

"They will assuredly rally to my cause. Long eons have they been imprisoned. They shall jump at the opportunity to wreak vengeance. With them by my side we shall sweep away the Olympians."

"And afterwards, oh liege?"

"Afterwards? They will gratefully resume their previous roles, only now with myself at their head.

" 'Godling', they mocked," Zeno whispered, lost in his thoughts of glory. "Soon I shall be referred to as 'Lord'!"

His master's mind on other things at the moment, Trepat let his eyes wander across the horizon. It was several seconds before he noticed a black dot far out to sea, but getting steadily closer.

"Ship ahoy!" was the shout by one of the sailors.

At this Zeno ceased his musings. "What ho, Captain?" he asked of their host.

Hobbling up, the rough-hewn salty dog squinted to make out the approaching vessel.

"Too far out. It may be a merchant or a fisherman. Perhaps even a returning ship of war. Then again, it could be—"

"Pirates!" the call rang out from the crowsnest, high on the ship's mast.

Now that the ship had come closer, all could see it clearly.

"The sails..." the captain noted grimly.

"What of them?"

"They are red."

As red as the blood that was no doubt spilt during the raids performed by those onboard.

"Perhaps they will leave us be," Trepat put in hopefully.

"Nay. They show 'the red' only when they are prepared to attack."

The sense of trepidation that had befallen the ship's crew seemed to touch Zeno not at all.

"I have paid good money for passage, Captain," he said, ignoring the oncoming menace. "I should think that would be sufficient to see us through, regardless of whatever jetsam and flotsam comes across our path."

The captain looked at him incredulously. Shaking his head, he bellowed to his crew. "Prepare to repel boarders!"

"Can we not flee?" Trepat asked, staring apprehensively at the oncoming vessel.

"The wind favors them," the captain answered distractedly. "They would be upon us ere we might escape. Nay," he continued, "our best chance lies in combating them. Pull, swine!" he suddenly yelled at his crew manning the oars. "I suggest that you make ready to fight." he finished, before moving on to see to further preparations.

"I shall not be denied!" Clinching a fist, Zeno shook it at the sky. "The gods seek to hinder, yet they shan't!"

In a half-daze, he allowed Trepat to lead him away.

***

"It takes a large man to admit when he was wrong. And I, Iochier the Great, am a large man." Iochier spread his arms and took a massive breath, his chest swelling to its limits before finally exhaling and giving it a final thump with his fist.

"The sea is everything you said, Glauce."

But the warring rhapsode heard him not, for her head was over the ship's side. Slightly green, she continued to 'feed the fish'. Despite her enthusiasm, her first taste of oceanic travel had not lived up to her expectations. Almost immediately, she had fallen ill. 'Sea sickness' the sailors called it.

"You will be fine," Heracles had assured her, slapping Glauce on the back jovially. "Once your 'sea legs' are underneath you, you will feel as yourself again."

While Glauce had taken a turn for the worse, Heracles' good humor had returned in full. Almost as soon as they were out of sight of Megera, he had returned to his boisterous self.

Xanthe alone seemed unaffected by the change in locale. But in truth, the long hours staring at the featureless plane had made her thoughtful.

Here she was, a mere mortal, on a quest for the gods themselves. As if that were not enough, there were her traveling companions. A villain to her people who turned out not to be villainous; a warrior who desired to not make war; and then there was Iochier (whom she had no idea about). It was quite the motley assemblage that the Fates had thrust together, and not one she would have thought likely beforehand.

"We make good time," Heracles stated, coming to join the Amazon at the ship's prow. "The winds favor us."

"A gift from the gods?"

Heracles shrugged. "Mayhap. It would behoove them to help us."

"I have wondered," Xanthe began, gazing out over the watery expanse, "to what extent may we depend upon their help? How far does Zeus' prohibition extend?"

Heracles stroked his beard contemplatively.

"I feel that father Zeus has set the game board and has decided to let the pieces set the pace."

"You think us pawns?"

"Was there ever a doubt?" the demigod grunted. "Such are the ways of my family."

With that, silence reigned, each lost to their own thoughts. So much so that it was some time before any of them noticed the small black speck against the vastness of the sea.

"What is that?" Iochier asked, pointing. "Another ship?"

"Nay," Heracles judged, shielding his eyes against the sun's glare. "And yet…"

"Ho, there are more!"

Sure enough, where before there had been one dot, there were now three. Then five, then seven. In no time at all, no less than a dozen black dots had appeared. And they were becoming more than mere dots as they approached.

"They are too fast for ships," Heracles pointed out. "Mark their speed. They glide through the sea like eels, or—"

"Sea serpents!"

***

"Ramming speed!"

A moment later, the pirate ship slammed into the galley, the ram shaped implement on its prow crashing into them amidships, throwing all and sundry to the decks. And before any could get to their feet, the attack began, the pirates swarming over the conjoined decks to wreak havoc.

There was no hiding or running, only the endless water waiting to claim those to whom misfortune's lot had been cast.

Trepat pulled his sword, the thrall intent on protecting his master, only to have Zeno lower his arm.

"Opportunity is oft mistaken for adversity," he remarked cryptically.

"Master?"

"Put away your sword, Trepat."

All around them the battle raged. The flash of bronze on bronze; the sound of men's voices raised in anger; the smell of blood and brine as both washed over the deck; it all assaulted the senses.

Though as far back at the stern as possible, Trepat feared that they would be set upon at any moment. But Zeno held a look of passivity, as if all that went on were but a show in an amphitheatre.

Even as they watched, one of the ship's crew managed to duck underneath a vicious cut aimed at his head, only to have the pirate stab him with a knife held in the other fist.

Gasping, the sailor fell to his knees, his life's blood pumping out. He never even saw the deathblow as the pirate brought his sword down on the man's unprotected head, cleaving it like a melon; leaving behind only a sucking noise as the blade was yanked free.

Heedless of the gore that clung to his sandaled feet, the pirate walked over the still warm corpse, making a beeline for Trepat and Zeno.

"Hold." Zeno demanded, holding out an upraised hand.

Surprised, the pirate actually stopped.

"I would have words with your captain."

The pirate leered, his open gape revealing many rotten (and missing) teeth.

"The captain be preoccupied at the moment, but I am sure that Poseidon has time to see you at the bottom of the sea!"

Thrusting Trepat aside, Zeno brought up his blade, squarely meeting the attacking pirate's slash.

Not expected the resistance, the pirate was flatfooted as Zeno kicked out, catching the sea dog in the stomach.

Instantly he leaned over, winded. Taking advantage of the opening, Zeno did what he did best: stabbing an enemy in the back.

The deed done, he turned back to Trepat.

"Do put him over the side. It is not the River Styx, but I shan't think that he shall care…"

***

They were everywhere, surrounding the ship on all sides. Their writhing forms rising from the ocean to tower above the ship's mast.

Black, sleek, they seemed to absorb the sun's rays rather than be lit by them. Long sinuous necks covered in innumerable scales, crowned by the most ferocious of heads. Long and oblong like that of a snake, but a fierce jutting maw that, when opened, revealed row upon row of razor sharp teeth.

Holdovers of a bygone era, they now 'stood' before the flower of humanity and seemed, in their presence, to say that Man was not at the top of the food chain after all.

"Does this answer your question of godly assistance?" Heracles asked dryly.

Indeed it did. Had Poseidon been permitted to aid them, surely he would not have allowed these creatures to molest them. They were truly on their own.

The monsters kept pace with the ship, bobbing to and fro on the waves.

Glauce looked up, briefly, before hanging back over the side rail. Iochier, upon spying the monstrosities, had joined her.

"Only a dozen," Heracles noted, sounding disappointed.

"You would have preferred more?" Xanthe asked, even as she drew her sword, eyes fixed upon the serpents.

"I have a fondness for slaying snakes, ever since I was but a babe. Have you heard of the time Hera sent two serpents to strangle me while I slept in the cradle…?"

Xanthe smiled. Now she knew that Heracles was well and truly back to his 'old' self.

With speed that belied its girth, one of the monsters struck.

Equally as fast, Xanthe's sword arm flashed out, catching the pre-historic beast across its bony jaw. She felt the blade as it sank through the slimy exterior, finding at last the bone underneath.

But it had been no more than a glancing blow, serving only to cause the fiend to recoil, hissing in pain. The battle had been joined.

With a whoop, Heracles cast aside his club and bow, and thus naked of armaments, dove into the serpent-infested waters bare handed.

In an explosion of action, another of the beasts dove to the ship's deck, seeking to swallow Xanthe whole.

Diving to the deck, she narrowly avoided the serpentine mouth as it snapped the air where she had just stood.

Rolling to her feet, the warrior woman hacked at the gigantic head, sending up a spray of blood and scales.

Reacting in pain, the monster retreated—giving Xanthe time enough to take the advantage. Screaming a war cry, she leaped at the larger-than-life monstrosity, plunging her sword deep into the exposed trunk of the creature.

With both hands she grasped her hilt, hanging off the side of the mountain of flesh. Thrashing, the oversized eel tossed back and forth, trying to dislodge its unwanted passenger. But the Amazon held on grimly.

Suddenly, the creature began to submerge, and it was with a worried frown that Xanthe watched as the ocean rapidly approached, its watery environs not amiable to air breathers such as herself.

Scrabbling, she fought to free her sword, and thereby save herself from a wet grave. But the monster's slimy exterior would allow her no purchase.

When all seemed lost, the fickle hand of Fate interceded. As the serpent descended, he passed by the ship's side—and Xanthe felt something catch a hold of her.

Looking up, she found herself looking into Glauce's eyes. But the rhapsode was not alone, for behind, hanging onto *her*, was Iochier, serving as the last link in the human chain.

With but a split second to act, all three pulled with all of their combined might. Xanthe to free her weapon, Glauce and Iochier to free *her*.

The Amazon felt her sword tear free, leaving the horror alone to slip under the frothing waves.

Hauled aboard, the three collapsed into a heap on the deck.

"I thank you," Xanthe breathed. "Both of you."

Rising, she looked about. "How fares Heracles?"

But she need not concern herself, the Scion of Olympus was in his element—battle.

Like a horseman attempting to tame a stead, the demigod was perched on the back of one of the leviathans, his biceps bulging from the effort of locking around the animal's slippery neck.

The air was rent with the howls of both wind and waves, and as such did much to mask the hero's laughter. But there was no hiding the look of exhilaration that effused his face as he wrestled with the monster of the deep.

Hither and yon the serpent thrashed, but Heracles held on doggedly, increasing his vice like grip.

Panicking, the underwater terror sought to take to its native element, as had the one Xanthe dispatched. But unlike Xanthe, Heracles made no move to disengage.

His massive chest swelled as he filled his lungs with air, precious seconds before he was plunged underwater.

Over and over the creature rolled, all the while its rider held both his seat and his breath.

Topside, the ship's defenders were equally hard pressed.

Nearly half a score of the watery fiends yet remained, and they seemed intent on revenging their peers. Fangs as sharp as any daggers now sought them. Held at bay only by the equal sharpness of Man's blade.

"Iochier, your help, now!" Xanthe called over the noise. She stood protectively over Glauce, whose seasickness was too much to overcome, leaving her prostrate upon the deck, moaning.

"Uh, I, uh—"

"Now!"

Managing to free his sword, he came up beside the Amazon. Together, Xanthe with quick premeditated thrusts, and Iochier with wild erratic swings, they stood together against the horde.

"I fear that the odds favor the fiends!" Iochier said, giving vent to Xanthe's own private musings.

If it were so, it were so. But they would know what it was to trifle with a daughter of the Amazons!

It would seem that no one could stand in such a predicament and hope to survive. No one that is, save for the Son of Zeus.

For at that moment the demigod broke the ocean's surface, a smile on his face and the broken corpse of a serpent in his hands.

Despite herself, Xanthe smiled.

Using his godly strength, Heracles swung the dead beast like a flail.

Smack, it hit one of the marauding beasts. Stunned, it sank from sight.

Another swing and another hit. Soon the entire pack was routed, fleeing in fear of the man who struck them with their own kind.

Gladly, the demigod accepted help getting back on board. Soaking wet, and looking like a drowned dog, Heracles still exuded an aura of respectful power. Chest heaving, he gratefully took the towel offered him.

"That is more to my liking!"

"It was a reckless tact you took," Xanthe chided.

"Nay. What better place to beard a beast than in its own lair?" he retorted, grinning from ear to ear. "I would hear how you and yours fared, but first, food! Combat always brings forth hunger! Let us break out the larders—tonight we feast! Let tomorrow bring what it may, for today we live!"

CHAPTER 10

The dead littered the deck, awash not in seawater, but blood. Where there had before been the roar of battle, there was now only silence.

The fight had been brutal, and though it had seemed to last eons, in truth it had all been over in minutes.

In the end, only two remained of the ship's original accompaniment: Zeno and Trepat. As it was, they found themselves staring across from what remained of the pirate crew. The battle had taken a toll on them as well.

"Who is in charge?" Zeno asked, directing the question at the remaining pirates.

Grumbling, they stood milling around until one of them spoke.

"Captain's dead."

Zeno nodded. "It would seem that you are in need of a new one. And I so happen to be in need of a crew."

The implication hung in the air.

"Why you?" someone asked.

"I can offer gold…"

"What is to stop us from taking it from you?" A chorus of laughter arose.

"What of immortality? Can you take that from my dead body?"

The laughter stopped.

Zeno smiled. "Pray tell, are any of you familiar with the Golden Apples of Hera?"

***

"Land ho!"

The others stopped what they were doing and looked.

Sure enough, just as Iochier had said, there on the horizon, was land.

Sicily.

An hour later saw them docking at a strange foreign port. Though no longer among the Greek isles, after several days in an open ship over the unforgiving sea, any port seemed like home. Especially to Glauce.

As soon as the ship touched the pier, the rhapsode was off like a shot. Shoving aside one and all, she stumbled down the gangplank and sank to her knees on the rich volcanic sand.

"Land," she breathed reverently. Happily, she put her cheek to the earth, oblivious to the stares of the locals.

Xanthe did not fight the grin that crept over her face.

"Where are we?" Iochier queried, looking around uneasily.

"Katane," Heracles answered, soaking in the surroundings. "In the land of the Sicels."

He shrugged at Xanthe's quizzical look.

"You forget, I have been around."

"Heracles!"

Hand on the hilt of her sword, Xanthe saw a man come running towards them.

"They look as we do!" Iochier exclaimed upon his first sight of a Sicel. Glauce gave him a sharp nudge in the ribs. Wincing, he rubbed at them.

"Heracles!" the man repeated upon reaching them. After that, Xanthe was lost, the man's language being unfamiliar to her. A glance at Glauce showed that the rhapsode was as much in the dark as she. Yet Heracles appeared to hang on every word.

A booming laugh ringing out, the Son of Zeus put his arms around the Sicel's shoulders and presented the man.

"Allow me to introduce Salvatair, greatest metalworker on this isle."

The demigod translated for his friend's sake, who in turn shook his head.

"Of mortal men, perhaps," the dark haired man was quick to amend in his own tongue. His well-muscled shoulders shifted under the smock he wore, giving vent to his discomfort at such high praise.

"It does not do to boast of one's prowess in the very shadow of Mount Etna, my friend!"

Heracles merely smiled. "Fear not, Salvatair, Hephaestus is not an envious god. Like myself, he has felt Hera's injustice, and thus knows the folly of the gods.

"In fact, we have come to visit brother Hephaestus' abode."

Salvatair gave him a strange look.

"You are the second assemblage to have come forth to honor the God of the Mount. Is there a holiday that we are not aware of?"

The strongman's eyes narrowed. "Second?"

"Aye, another party of your countrymen were here, their leader a tall man of regal bearing. Pilgrims he said. Yet, when they were informed of Hephaestus' absence they pressed on all the same."

"What be the matter?" Xanthe asked, noting Heracles' change in attitude.

"It would seem that brother Zeno has beaten us here."

"How long?"

"Mere hours," Heracles translated.

"How far is Mount Etna?"

"Not more than thirteen or fourteen leagues."

"Are there steeds on this island?" Xanthe was all business.

Heracles shook his head. "Nay, naught but sturdy work ponies. Well enough for plowing, yet not suitable for speed."

Iochier spoke what was on everyone's mind.

"Then how are we to overtake the miscreants? We have lost afore we have even begun."

"What need have we of horse power when we have manpower at our disposal?" Heracles posited, cryptically.

The demigod rattled off something to Salvatair in his own language. Nodding, the Sicel ran off.

Xanthe raised an eyebrow, to which Heracles held up a finger, bidding her to wait. That the Amazon was content to do so was a mark of the respect she had begun to accord him.

Soon the Sicel was back, trailing behind him a handcart.

"Your chariot awaits," Heracles exclaimed, gesturing to the little wooden contraption. Dusty, and well worn, it looked exactly like what it was: a small two-wheeled cart meant for the conveyance of tools and crops.

Iochier was confused. "I see no horse..."

"You have no need of one when you have the aid of the Son of Zeus."

His biceps rippling, the muscles and tendons growing taunt, he flexed to showcase what he had in mind. A force of nature constrained only by a prison of semi-mortal flesh.

"You intend to pull us?"

"Aye," the Scion of Olympus confirmed, "and faster than any horse this side of Pegasus."

Xanthe did not miss a beat. Stepping aboard, she grasped the cart's sides, knowing the kind of ride they were in for.

Once Iochier and Glauce joined her, Heracles thanked his friend and then set off.

With a speed that surprised, Heracles ran, a cloud of dust being left in his wake.

Bounding along the uneven ground, the little cart jumped and jolted over every rut, pothole, and rock Nature saw fit to put in its path. As such, it was not long before Glauce was hanging over the side, one hand holding the cart in a death grip, the other clutching Iochier for balance.

"It is as though we were back on the ship!" she moaned.

***

"What do you make of that?" the pirate asked his companion, pointing to the rapidly approaching dust cloud.

Squinting, the other was unable to make any more sense of it.

"Avast ye dogs! What be the matter?" another asked, coming over to see what was holding them up. "You are falling behind!"

"Yonder," the first pirate said, pointing. "What is that?"

"Who cares?"

At this point Zeno himself showed up, in no good mood at having the march stalled.

"Gentlemen, the mount is *before* us, not aft!"

"There is a storm brewing, or some such."

Looking for himself, Zeno saw the cloud. At first he thought that his eyes were playing tricks on him, yet even when he looked away and then back, it remained.

"There is be a dust storm coming," he lied. "Such are common here. It is best that we make camp, lest it overtake us on the road. Let it waste its fury while we are hunkered and ready for it, and upon the morrow we can start anew."

Never ones to overlook the chance at shirking work, the pirates agreed that it was a sound plan, and waited not at all to implement it. All the while the dust came steadily closer.

After their cohorts settled down for the coming onslaught, and all was silent, Zeno tapped Trepat on the shoulder, and with his head indicated that they were leaving. Now.

The pirates or the coming 'storm', it mattered not who survived. In the end there could be only one. And that was himself.

***

They burst upon the pirates before they were even aware of them. Xanthe did not know who was more surprised.

The only one who was not caught flatfooted was Heracles. Rather than coming to a stop, he continued straight on, barreling through the bandits like the storm they had thought him to be.

Left and right they flew; some to avoid the cart, others because they were unable to do so.

Finally screeching to a halt, the demigod left off his role as pack animal, and instead hefted his great war club, swinging it in a tight arc.

"Have at thee, base curs!"

Not as theatric, Xanthe thrust her sword between the ribs of the nearest of the foemen—dropping him to the ground without a sound.

It was a good thing that they held the element of 'shock and awe', for Glauce was not yet recovered. She still swayed, though they had stopped. One hand grabbed at the cart, the other, her head.

For his part, Iochier stood about her, indecisive as to whether to stay with the rhapsode or go help his comrades.

As Fate would have it, his aid would not be needed.

Rearing back, Heracles gave a mighty swing, catching two pirates with but a single blow.

Beside him, Xanthe parried one blade while dodging another, and before either could recover, the Amazon sent a roundhouse kick to one's face. And using momentum, she executed a one-handed handspring, striking the other attacker, knocking him to the ground.

Both made easy targets for her thirsty sword.

Thinking there to be safety in numbers, half a dozen pirates rushed at them en masse.

Meeting them half way, Heracles scattered them aside with his war club as if they were mere flies.

And as the bones and gore flew, so too did Xanthe, charging amongst them with a gleam in her eye matched only by the play of sunlight upon her sword.

A vicious chop nearly took off one of the pirate's heads; only a hasty block had prevented it. But such was the ferocity of the Amazon's swing that the clanging of the blades had forced his own to rebound and bounce off of his forehead. Not a killing blow, but it left blood to stream into his eyes.

Eyes that failed to see the knee that struck him in the groin. Groaning, he collapsed into a bloodied heap.

"Who be next on the docket?" Xanthe asked, motioning to the others.

None seemed particularly eager.

"Come, do you wish to live forever?"

That seemed to galvanize them. They came at her like a wave. Yet, like a wave, they soon found themselves crashing against the rock that was the blonde battler.

Dropping low, the warrioress did the splits—then from her vantage point split a pirate at the knees. Screaming, he suddenly found himself shorter by half.

Twisting like a top, the Amazon tripped the nearest man. And before he could regain his feet, she had sprung upon him, thrusting her sword down into his exposed back.

It was a killing blow as well as an aid to regaining her feet.

Scarcely had she pulled the crimson blade free when she jumped over the still cooling corpse and slammed into another attacker shoulder first. Staggering, he reeled into a fellow, and thus started a domino effect that would throw off the entirety of the body of men.

Leaping at the opportunity, Xanthe lashed out with abandon. Feinting left, she would attack from the right. Kicks to the chest, jabs to the face, all were the same to one steeped in the arts of war, such as herself.

Riding the thrill of battle, she suddenly found herself squaring off with two separate foes, their single thought being to take advantage of her divided attention.

She did not even bother to wipe away the blood that flecked her features. Features that, had they not been arranged in a frightening grimace of war, would have set the men's hearts to pounding for an entirely different reason.

Both parties licked their lips. Theirs out of nervousness, hers out of anticipation.

Cheeks flushed, breast heaving, she would have been a vision of loveliness in another setting. But here and now she appeared to the sea rats as a hungry shark, eager for a meal.

"Boo!"

Panicked, the pirates broke and ran.

Xanthe smiled.

As did Heracles. These were bandits, not trained warriors. There were no tactics or strategy needed here, just unorganized savagery. Which suited the demigod just fine.

A man's ribs here, another's head there; it was melee combat without any pretence at elegance. And if there was one thing that the Scion of Olympus detested, it was pretense.

While the two weapon masters were kept busy, some of the gang tried their hands at what they thought were the easier pickings: Iochier and Glauce.

Iochier swallowed as he noted a couple of pirates converging on them. Yanking his sword from his sheath, he brandished it about as menacingly as he could.

"Halt, miscreants!" he shouted, his voice cracking only a little.

The pirates laughed.

"Run," Glauce croaked, barely able to hold her head up. It was an order, not a suggestion. He shot her a sharp look.

"And leave you alone? Whom do you have the least regard for: yourself or me?"

Iochier could not tell if the look on her face was one of surprise or upset stomach.

Like hyenas sensing weakness, the pirates pounced. But then a funny thing happened. Namely, Iochier slipped and fell.

Bracing to meet the rush, he had shifted his feet, and in doing so stepped on a loose rock, which in turn caused him to lose his balance and fall flailing to the ground.

The result of which was his being spared a killing blow by a pirate's axe, and instead tripping the attacker.

Tangled and twisted, the two fought in the dirt. Not only for the upper hand, but to extradite themselves. Like dogs, they rolled around, struggling and straining.

In so doing, Iochier's helmeted head came into contact with the pirate's un-helmeted one, knocking the pirate out and wedging Iochier's helm down over his eyes.

As such, he was in no position to see the other ruffian bearing down on him.

Desperately trying to get his helmet unstuck, he heard a sharp *thud*. Yanking it off, he saw Glauce, staff in hand, standing over the limp form of a pirate.

"I feel much better now," the rhapsode asserted, smiling.

CHAPTER 11

In the aftermath, all felt a sense of satisfaction, save for Xanthe, who noticed that Zeno was not amongst the lot.

"What are we to do with them?" Glauce asked, assaying the broken and battered sea scum.

The demigod smiled. "Worry not about them, little one. The natives are not favorable to strangers. Especially such as these. I suspect that they shall get that which is their due."

"Let us make haste."

As far as Xanthe was concerned, the pirates were yesterday's news, they were no longer a viable threat. The real threat was currently on his way to Mount Etna.

Glauce looked to the handcart and then to her fellow sword sister. "In that?" it was more of a plea than a question.

"In that."

Sighing bitterly, the rhapsode piled into the cart with the rest.

Heracles, once more doubling as an ox, pulled them along with all speed towards the mountain.

***

Zeno stumbled over the rock strewn slope. Behind him, Trepat stared in awe. The mountain's very top was lost within a mass of swirling mist—or were they clouds? Either way, the summit was hidden from mortal eyes. Truly, the home of a god.

Zeno took out the Key of Hephaestus, its subtle pull telling him the way to the secret entrance.

While slow going, they went higher and higher, the air becoming progressively thinner and colder.

"Not… Much…. Farther…" Zeno panted, forcing his feet to doggedly shamble onwards.

Trepat refrained from replying, instead turning his energy towards keeping up with his master.

"Here!"

Looking up, the servant saw Zeno standing still, the Key extended before him, straining to leave his hand, pointing directly at a nondescript portion of blank mountainous rock.

"Here!" the demigod repeated, his eyes fixated on the spot. "The secret door is here!"

Placing the artifact against the cold stone, he could feel, as well as hear, a low rumbling sound emanating from somewhere deep inside the mountain.

And as he stood transfixed, he saw the mountain's face shift and change, as it might in a dream. Where there had but a moment before stood blank rock, now was an open portal to the recesses of the great smithy's inner workshop.

Without preamble, the would-be-god strode through, leaving Trepat scrambling to follow.

***

"How… far…" Iochier gasped, unable to finish the sentence.

Crawling up the mountainside like ants on a tree, the chill atmosphere conspired to rob the breath from their lungs.

Glauce too labored to continue; yet they had only to look to Xanthe and Heracles to find the strength to go on. The Amazon and the demigod bent to their task as though they were part goat.

"Not much farther," Heracles answered, not breaking his stride. "Zeno's trail is obvious enough for Homer himself to see."

Heracles' confidence aside, Xanthe knew that they needed to find Zeno (and the hidden entrance) soon—night was beginning to fall. And she did not relish trying to survive out in the elements at this altitude once the cold settled in.

Clambering over yet another rock, the Amazon stopped in mid stride. Straightening, she squinted her eyes, her gaze focusing on something.

"Heracles," the woman warrior called out, "There," she pointed to the blank stone. "Do you see anything amiss?"

Studying the scene before him, Heracles gradually made out a patch of darkness not as dark as the rest.

Though his features were hidden in the gathering gloom, the mirth in the demigod's voice could not be mistaken. "Aye, I think that we have before us the secret way."

"It is open, which can mean only one thing: that Zeno is inside even now."

Spurred to greater effort, the group entered the mountain.

Making their way through the living rock, they noticed a substantial change in temperature. Whereas outside it had been cold (and was getting colder), here it was warm. In fact, the farther they walked into the narrow, winding tunnel, the warmer it became.

It also became lighter. Soon they could see their own shadows flickering across the stonewalls.

Iochier started to say something before Xanthe cut him off with a gesture. The implication was clear: quiet was called for here. They had no idea what they were up against.

Rounding a bend, they were suddenly thrust into the midst of a truly gargantuan cavern.

All the imaginings of Glauce's flights of fancy had not prepared her for the magnificence of such a sight.

Towering so far above their heads as to be lost from sight, were terraces, carved by an expert hand into the very sides of the mountain; each and every one of them filled willy-nilly with items the likes of which mortal eyes had never seen.

Suits of armor of a metal none of them could name; weapons so large that only a giant or a god could have wielded them; strange wheeled conveyances that sputtered and vented steam; metal automatons that walked by way of an odd key thrust into their back. A strange, bewildering, and not more than a little unnerving, array of godly contraptions that assaulted the senses.

And there, in the very center of the complex, the source of the light that filled the insides of the mountain—not to mention the now nearly stifling temperature. An enormous hole, surrounded by a railing, and in it, the true secret of Mount Etna.

It was not a mountain at all, but a volcano.

The molten core bubbled and churned, the very heart of it giving off the distinctive glow that infused the underground workshop. Truly this was the ultimate smithy for the ultimate craftsman.

Glauce put a hand to her head, as much as to wipe away the perspiration on her brow as to signify her overwhelmed state at the sights before her.

"Amazing."

Even Xanthe was nonplused. It seemed like an eternity before she managed to tear away her gaze and remind them all of the task at hand.

Deciding that it was better to move as one unit, the group cautiously made their way across the treasure filled vault.

"Where does Hephaestus store the Thunderbolts he makes for Zeus?" Glauce whispered.

"That I know not," Heracles answered. "Though, knowing brother Hephaestus' dislike for pomp, doubtless they are in some cluttered corner amongst his other works, undistinguished."

Iochier craned his neck, looking at the multiple levels of the cavern. "We could search for days and not find them."

"We need not find *them*," Xanthe corrected, "we need only find he whom seeks them: Zeno."

***

Trepat looked about, wide-eyed in awe. "By the gods…"

"One god in fact," Zeno clarified, moving aside a bronze globe, undeterred by anything save what he sought, leaving it to Trepat to gaze wonderingly upon the divinely wrought artifact.

So round, a perfect sphere. It was a globe of sorts, but one unlike any he had ever seen. There were lands indicated where none should be. After all, whoever heard of an entire continent at the bottom of the world?

"They are here," the would-be-god said, recapturing his servant's attention. "I can feel them. Thunderbolts fit for a god," he laughed. "It is ironic that Zeus' own weapons should bring about his downfall!"

***

Iochier stood admiring a finely crafted statue of what was surely one of the gods, such was its proportion and grace, and was about to bring it to Glauce's attention when they heard the sound of laughter.

***

"This grows monotonous," Zeno huffed, peering yet again around yet another fabulous artifact to no avail.

"Trepat, if you were the God of the Forge, where might you keep—" he started to ask before noting that Trepat was nowhere to be found. "Trepat." he called out. "Trepat!"

Trepat winced at the summons. "Over here, my lord."

"Why have you—"

"Master," the servant begged, cutting him off, "I thought that I heard a noise from down there," he pointed to one of the innumerable recesses in the cavern.

Concerned, Zeno looked back. "We must hurry."

Throwing caution to the wind, he began to throw things. Following his master's lead, Trepat cast about as well, both heedless of the amount of noise they were making.

***

Racing around a massive structure, Glauce turned to her sword sister. "What is the plan?" She asked, cloak flapping behind her whizzing frame.

"Find Zeno. Kill Zeno. Return home."

"Some plan." Iochier panted, struggling to keep up.

"It is simple enough." Heracles admitted. "I like it." Flashing a grin, he put on a burst of speed and passed them all.

***

"My liege…"

"I know, Trepat, I know," Zeno answered the unspoken plea. The forces of the old order were nearly at hand. They who would deny him, and the world, the destiny intended for them both. It must not be!

"Zeno!" Heracles' voice reverberated throughout the rocky abode. "Your mad quest is at an end. If you give up now, mayhap it shall go lightly for you. Though not likely." he added, not without mirth.

Zeno said nothing, rather, he redoubled his searching.

***

"Surely he knows that there can be no escape," Iochier exclaimed as he picked his way carefully amongst the workshop's wonders.

"Such as he do not yield easily," Glauce explained. "Note the extreme measures that brought him to this place. Nay, one of his ambitions will not accept defeat meekly."

Crouching down, Xanthe addressed her comrades.

"Now is the time to divide our forces. We know that he is here, and we must find him ere he finds the Thunderbolts. Heracles and I will take this direction," she gestured as though cutting a pie.

"And it is left to us take the other," Glauce finished.

Xanthe nodded. "Aye. We shall meet halfway. Between us we will flush out our prey."

***

"The Thunderbolts could be anywhere," Trepat's anxiety was showing. "How are we to find them before we ourselves are found?"

If they did not procure the Thunderbolts soon, all would be lost. And Zeno doubted not Heracles' dim view on his treatment at the hands of the gods. An eternity in Tarturas flashed through his mind. Disturbed, he shook the image away.

No, the Thunderbolts had to be found.

***

"Hurry, this way," Glauce tossed back over her shoulder, careful not to lose her stride. "The noise is emanating from over here."

"Slowly," her companion puffed. "It is not as though he is going anywhere."

"A moment wasted is a moment closer he is to his goal," the rhapsode reproached. "Speed is of the essence."

"I thought it was stealth that was called for?"

"It was," she answered, "however, that was before. Now it is speed."

"You are making this up as you go along, are you not?" he accused.

"Less speaking, more speeding."

***

The noise was unmistakable: someone was doing their level best to avoid Xanthe and her troop. Good. It meant that their quarry was perhaps panicking. If so, he would be all the easier to deal with.

Ducking, the Amazon avoided the outstretched arm of a statue. It was only a matter of time now.

***

He could hear them coming. His breathing became more rapid, as he frantically scanned the isles of godly artifices for the one treasure that stood above the rest.

Hearing a shuffling to his left, he darted into a golden goblet large enough to hold three grown men. Careful not to move a muscle, he listened intently.

Footfalls. Not so much heard as *felt* through the metallic base of his hiding place.

Steady. Deliberate. Confident. The tread of a hunter. And him the prey!

And not far off, another set of footsteps. Not nearly so measured, without even the pretense of silence.

He lay there, waiting as the seconds stretched on. Only when he was sure that they had gone did he dare peek up over the rim. Seeing the way clear, he clamored out of his hiding place to silently pad along his way.

"Over there!" Glauce shouted, seeing the tail end of the fleeting figure. Extra spring to her step, the redhead flew into action.

"Cut him off!" she yelled to Iochier.

Struggling to do just that, the warrior's mismatched armor sang and clanged like a blacksmith's forge. In addition to being loud, it also served to slow him down.

Skidding around an ornate mirror fit for a queen, Glauce just managed to see the trailing foot of the man as he raced behind another aisle of workings.

"Over there," she informed Iochier when he showed up, huffing and puffing.

"What now?" he asked, hands on his knees, chest heaving.

"We follow."

"Of course…"

The rhapsode could not tell if he was being sarcastic or not. Eying him for good measure, she led the way.

His head on a swivel, the 'warrior prince' could not help but be in awe.

"These products are fabulous. The precision necessary…"

"You should be looking for Zeno. Not admiring baubles," Glauce retorted sharply.

"Is that a Muse's Pen?"

"Where?" The woman's head whipped around sharply, her eyes searching.

Iochier wore a sly grin.

Flustered, she turned back to the task at hand.

***

He could hear their banter, and that was good. Stationed as he was on top of an enormous set of scales, (no doubt intended for the God of Justice) he was in a prime position to take out two birds with one stone.

Cautious, the duo advanced, the way too narrow for anything other than single file.

"It is quiet," Iochier noted, his gaze wary.

"Too quiet."

On edge, both had an odd feeling suddenly grip them. Not a premonition so much as a pre-natural sense of their surroundings. A warrior's instinct.

"Move!" they both yelled at the same time, each trying to shove the other away, the result being that both went careening, even as a giant scale came crashing down, sending debris flying.

Shaken, but unharmed, Glauce got up. Where she had stood a moment before, the stone floor showed a spider web of cracks, such had been the force with which the scales had hit. The rhapsode gave thanks that Justice was indeed blind.

"Iochier!" she exclaimed, remembering her companion. Yet, even as she looked for him, there he was, struggling with his helmet, it having gotten stuck over his eyes—again.

Holding her laughter in check, she went and aided him. With his sight restored, he beheld how close they had come to being crushed.

"On the *balance*, I would say that we were lucky."

Glauce rolled her eyes and let the pun pass.

Shaking her head, Glauce led the way again, but by now their prey had sufficient time to make his getaway.

***

"You would be King of the Gods? Then show us your mettle!" Heracles challenged impatiently. "If you have the stones to usurp father Zeus, then surely you can not fear mites such as us!"

There was no response to his taunts. Xanthe distrusted the silence.

***

He could see them. Such arrogance. That they dared to question his valor. Seething, he had to check his impulse to rush out and meet their brazen challenge. But now was not the time to fight. Now was the time to *find*.

***

A noise—the sound of a man running away.

"He flees!" She raced after the sound.

All else was shut out, save the rhythmic pounding of her heart as she gave chase. She would neither tire nor flag in her effort. As the hound ran the fox to the ground, so would she corner this cosmic upstart.

***

He could tell that she was following him. Good. It was a strategy as old as warfare itself: divide and conquer. With her cut off and alone, she would be easier to take.

***

Just ahead she saw a quick flash of movement around a magnificent bust of Aphrodite. She put on a burst of speed, but instead of going around the corner upright, she went into a forward roll. Some sixth sense had nagged at her, and a good thing too.

The sword strike that followed would have taken off her head otherwise. As it was, the bronze weapon rebounded from the statue instead, breaking off the goddess' arms. Strangely, it looked better that way.

Leaping to her feet, the huntress set about bagging her quarry. But he did not seem eager to cooperate.

Jumping backwards, she avoided a renewed attempt at her head. Feinting with a jab, she launched a crosscut at her opponent's exposed thigh.

Twisting, he barely avoided the blow. Using his spin's momentum, he threw out a backhanded slash, the sword whistling as he arched through the air.

Ducking, she thrust with her own weapon. Unable to avoid the attack, it sank deep within his gut.

His eyes wide, his mouth open, he sank to his knees in both pain and shock. To have been bested by a woman…

As she stood over her vanquished foe, Iochier came into view, waving his sword about in an absurd manner.

"You did it," he said approvingly.

"Was there ever a doubt?" Glauce answered, smugly.

It was with justifiable pride that the rhapsode looked on as Trepat gasped for air.

A staff to the stomach seldom failed to produce the desired results.

***

Slowly, Xanthe picked her way through the cavern, careful not to make a sound. She was on the right trail, she just *felt* it.

Zeno too could feel it, the inextricable closing of the net. But he did not panic. Already the forces arrayed against him had been divided, and divided again. Once he eliminated this blonde haired wench, there would be one less pursuer to worry about.

He waited, allowing her to come to him, like the spider and the fly. The trap was laid, and the bait was set. It was so simple that it could not fail.

Even as the thought crossed his mind, his intended victim came into view.

The way looked clear. There were several weapons racks gleaming dully in the lava-light, all together they made up an aisle.

Treading carefully, Xanthe placed one foot in front of the other, muscles tense, sword arm ready to deal death when needed.

A clatter from behind. Spinning, the Amazon cut with her sword in a defensive manner, intending to parry the thrust or cut that she expected. Only, there was nothing to defend against.

She spied on the floor a lone spear having somehow worked itself free of the rack it had resided in.

She would have cursed herself a fool, except that she saw by the flickering light a reflection in the polished metal head of the fallen weapon. A reflection that was not her own.

Throwing herself aside, she could feel the sparks created by her would be killer's sword striking the polished stone floor.

Without leaving her crouch, Xanthe struck out at Zeno's legs, hoping to bring him down to her level—the hard way.

Desperately, he brought his knees up, but the short hop was not enough to avoid the Amazon's body as it crashed into him. Off balance, they both tumbled to the floor.

With a speed born of self-preservation, Zeno's hands flew up to claw at Xanthe's face. The struggle had been reduced to one of mere animal ferocity.

Bringing up a knee, the blond battler tried to hit the demigod where it counted. But at the last moment he shifted position, causing the blow to land wide.

Around they rolled until they banged into one of the weapon racks, sending it topping over with a resounding *crash*.

A falling mace striking her a glancing blow, Xanthe was momentarily dazed as Zeno scrambled to his feet, intent on finding a weapon with which to end this, when his attention was arrested.

The falling rack had revealed it. A simple bronze urn, unadorned, plainly constructed. But lying inside of it, like arrows in a quiver, were what he had come for: The Thunderbolts of Zeus.

Jagged, vibrant with energy, they pulsed with their own inner light. Living lightning. Their power was palpable.

Almost reverently, he walked to them, the fight forgotten. Each step as unsteady as his own mind.

Coming to, Xanthe saw the situation for what it was. Getting to her feet, she made a dash at intercepting him.

Only then did the demigod become aware of his dire plight.

Franticly, he raced towards the Thunderbolts, Xanthe only a few steps behind. He felt her hand on his shoulder even as he boldly grabbed at one of the heavenly bolts.

In that moment his entire being seemed infused with power. As though he had become a Thunderbolt himself. His very body glowed with an aura.

Dismayed, Xanthe saw his hand grip the divine bolt.

And then the world ended.

CHAPTER 12

The sound alone was enough to bring everyone to their knees. Everyone that is, expect Zeno.

In the midst of it all he stood triumphant.

Some distance away lay Xanthe. Unconscious and bleeding, the Amazon had been tossed like a rag doll by the sonic explosion.

Now *this* was power. Zeno looked at the instrument in awe. Hephaestus did good work. Perhaps he would be kept on after Zeno's ascension, if only to create more Thunderbolts.

The demigod laughed as he hefted the urn containing the cosmic bolts. Striding confidently back the way he had come, he noticed Trepat sprawled upon the floor unconscious, surrounded by his captors.

"Come," he said, reviving his fallen servant, "it is time that we made our leave. There is much left to accomplish."

"What of the others, my liege?"

Zeno smiled. They had proven to be but bugs before his might. How much better would it be to deal with them as such?

Gaining the stairs, the duo made their way to freedom, picking their way down the mountain. The moonshine cast more than enough illumination for their purposes.

Making sure that they were well away from the mountain, Zeno slipped a mystic bolt from the urn, its glow reflecting the manic light in its new owner's eyes as he took aim and cast the godly implement towards the now distant mound.

The sky and the rock screamed out in unison as an entire side of the mountain exploded, sending debris raining down for leagues and leagues around.

Like a living thing, the mountain sought to heal its gaping wound. Only, instead of blood, it oozed molten rock. An avalanche, the likes of which few had ever seen, sought to fill in the gaping hole Zeno had wrought.

***

It seemed as though the entire mountain was coming down about their heads.

Large chunks of stone came crashing down, destroying priceless works of art, not to mention threatening the lives of those within.

The walls slid as though turned to liquid, the floors cracked, sending fissures throughout the entire complex. Even the mountain's molten core had become excited, boiling and bubbling away, threatening to overflow.

The Workshop of the Gods would be in dire need of some work itself.

Yet despite the destruction, Zeno's goal had not been achieved. Though battered, bruised, and bloody, they still lived. As did their desire.

"When next we meet, I shall wear his innards for a necklace," Xanthe vowed grimly, wiping away the blood and grime that covered her face.

"Easier to say than to make so," Glauce responded, frowning at the shambles around them. "Yon entrance is blocked. How are we to take up the chase anew? Wait until Hephaestus returns?"

"I should not like to explain this to him…" Iochier put in, his gaze sweeping over the devastation.

"There be no need," Heracles pronounced, rubbing the back of his head.

"Then how are we to leave?"

The others watched as the demigod looked around. His gaze stopped at one spot on the far wall. Smiling, he walked over to it and stood there a moment, sizing it up. Then, clenching his right hand into a fist, he gave a whoop and struck the mountain as though it were a mortal foe.

Like a piston, he continued to strike, again and again as the others looked on amazed.

A tunnel was forming. He worked away at it in such a manner for some hours, until finally there could be felt a cool breeze upon their cheeks as he broke through to the outside.

"Ah," Glauce sighed, "that feels wonderful."

Xanthe, however, had her mind on other matters,

"He has regained his lead. If we are to bridge it, we must depart this isle as soon as possible."

"To where?"

"The Immortal Grove of Hera."

***

Though they did indeed hasten, the pace seemed all too slow to Xanthe. By the time were under way, the blond battler was in a right old snit.

She had had Zeno in her sights; a mere moment more and she could have ended all of this. The feeling of abject failure gnawed at her.

She sat alone at the ship's forecastle. Or at least as alone as one could aboard ship.

Heracles manned the tiller, regaling a rapt Iochier with tales of daring do.

"—there I be. Burdened with the weight of the cosmos upon my shoulders. Atlas had gone off, and I stood there alone with naught but my own dark thoughts of his not returning."

"Yet he did return," Iochier said, leaning forward eagerly, despite knowing the tale.

"Aye, and a good thing too. Else I would still be trapped on that far distant shore, spending my days holding up the sky. The tedium alone would have been maddening."

As Xanthe sat watching the waves roll in and out in an unending motion as old as the world itself, her mind cast back over her life as an Amazon. Her training, her sense of determination, came once more to the fore.

"You are an Amazon," she seemed to hear the voice of her queen say, as she had been wont to when in the presence of novices, "your strength comes from your unity. Alone we are capable of only so much. Yet together, oh, together we are capable of so much more. A campaign is waged by many, not one."

It was a truism, and one that Xanthe had forgotten. They all had their parts to play. Their numbers gave them strength, whereas Zeno's singularity put him at a disadvantage. There were many hounds, but one fox.

"Ho, Xanthe," called Heracles, "rouse yourself from your morose disposition. Your gloom spreads to yon rhapsode."

A sweat drenched head rose up from the deck, its eyes going in and out of focus.

Xanthe hid a smile. "I suspect that the reasons for her gloom are different from my own."

Even as she said it, Glauce lurched to her feet and barely cleared the side before emptying her stomach yet again.

Her mind settled for the moment, the Amazon set her gaze once more upon the distant horizon. Noting only vaguely the gathering of clouds far away.

***

Zeno struggled with the sail, fighting the ever increasing wind, even as Trepat sought to keep an even till in the now choppy sea.

It had been more difficult to obtain transportation than Zeno had anticipated. Not only was he unable to speak the local language, but certain of the crew he had landed with were being rounded up, which did not make outlanders the most popular of people at the moment.

Such being the case, he was lucky to have been able to steal a fisherman's boat. A sorry way to ride into immortality, but it would have to serve.

The demigod bit back a curse, a storm was brewing, there could be no doubt about it now. Yet, to think that a bit of rain and wind would bring him to heel was laughable. The gods themselves had proven powerless to stop him. Let the elements rage, he would soon be their master!

***

The wind had gone from a gust, to a breeze, to a gale. The storm front had come in, blotting out the sun, turning the sky into a roiling mass of gray. Rain came lashing down, soaking everyone to the bone.

The craft lurched like a toy in some child's tub, battered to and fro. North, South, East, West, it seemed to come from all directions at once. What the rain failed to get to, the waves did as they sloshed over the sides, making one's footing perilous. Each moment a struggle against being pitched over into the frothing waters.

It was all Glauce could do to hold onto the mainmast. With a death like grip, she clung to it, even as she fell in and out of consciousness.

Next to her lay Iochier. Twice already he had gone overboard, barely plucked from a watery grave at the last instant.

At last he was lashed to the rhapsode, and together they rode out Nature's fury.

As for Xanthe herself, she stood vigil at the ropes, desperately trying to haul the sail down, lest the storm tear it to shreds.

And at the tiller was Heracles, his laughter lost in the roar of the wind.

"*This* is living!"

As Xanthe fought her own battle, she felt a shifting under her feet. Chancing a glance, she noted that the ship was rising, as though on wings.

With mounting dread, she gave the situation her full attention, and was sorry that she had.

The ship was rising on the curl of a wave twice the height of their craft. As soon as they reached its peak…

"Hold on!" the Amazon screamed as they hit the crest. From then it was a lesson in Physics. Namely, that what goes up must come down.

As though dropped from the hand of a giant, the ship came crashing back down, hitting with such force as to nearly jar Heracles loose from his seat. But rather than anger or fear, he instead felt exhilarated. Things were just beginning to get good!

***

Zeno had given up any hope of control long ago. The open fishing boat rode one massive wave after another, each time settling a little lower in the water.

The storm had long since claimed the tiny craft's sail, and now was seeking the rest of it.

Thinking quickly, Trepat had lashed both himself and his master to the now barren mast. It was not much, but it kept them from being swept away.

No sail, no rudder, no anything, they were forced to bob like a piece of cork on the increasingly brutal sea.

The rain stung his face even as he sought to shield his master. But from the forces of nature, there would be no shielding.

***

The ocean churned, the heavens wailed, and all was confusion and chaos. To be caught in such a maelstrom would mean doom to the poor unfortunate. As though between the hammer and the anvil, all was smashed flat as the callous voice of the storm shrieked its supremacy.

CHAPTER 13

The inky abyss had grown lighter by degrees until finally it became a bright light hammering at her eyelids. Forcing the sea-salt encrusted orbs open, Xanthe squinted against the sun's incandescent rays. She sought to raise her hand to blot it out, only to immediately regret it as her head throbbed in time with the movement.

It was some minutes before she regained a measure of her strength to try again, and this time she raised herself up on one elbow to take stock of her surroundings.

She was on a beach. The last thing she remembered was the ship capsizing.

All along the shore were pieces of wood, the remnants of the craft. But what of the crew?

Forcing herself to her feet, her aching limbs screaming in protest, she knew that she had to find out what had become of her cohorts.

Following the trail of debris, she became increasingly worried. On one hand, seeing nothing was a good sign—no bloated corpses. But on the other, nothing was still nothing.

She combed the beach until fatigue set in. Sitting down to rest, the Amazon was despondent.

Her allies—gone. Zeno—gone. Her transportation—gone. And to top it all off, she was now cast upon some distant shore with no idea as to where to go.

The blond took her head in her hands, to ease its incessant pounding if nothing else.

"It is a fine thing. We spend half the morning searching hither and yon for you, and here you are resting as though on holiday!"

Though her head objected to so violent a motion, Xanthe whipped it around and beheld the smiling face of Heracles. And beside him, worse for wear, but certainly alive, were Glauce and Iochier.

The rhapsode nursed an injured rib, as Iochier shifted an arm in a makeshift sling.

"It does my heart good to see you safe," Glauce said to Xanthe, smiling every bit as much as the demigod.

"As it does mine," Iochier seconded, wincing slightly as he instinctively attempted to raise the injured arm in greeting.

"We live," the warrior woman noted simply.

"Aye, and it is a good thing too," Heracles said, folding his bare arms in front of his massive chest. He at least had made it through the ordeal unscathed. "While I have known a sea nymph or two in my time, I have no desire to set up permanent housekeeping with them."

Xanthe rose to her feet and clasped the demigod's arm by way of formal greeting; such was her pleasure in seeing him alive.

"Where are we?" she asked.

"I have not the slightest of ideas," he admitted. "Let us find out."

"How?" Iochier asked, trying to be still as Glauce fussed with his sling.

"We are on the coast," Glauce said, concentrating on her handiwork. "It stands to reason that there must be a port somewhere. And where there is a port—"

"—there are people." Xanthe finished.

The Amazon looked anew at the reformed group. They had no provisions; those had been lost with the ship. Their weapons however, had survived with them, so that was a plus. It was also all important, considering that they knew not if the natives were friendly.

Bedraggled and careworn, the Greek adventurers set out along their sandy path, mindful of what may lie ahead.

***

Trepat was tending to the fire when his master awoke. Hurriedly, he came to Zeno's side, helping the latter up to a sitting position.

"I live," he laughed, weakly.

"Aye, Master."

"A fire?" Zeno questioned, seeing the blaze.

"Aye. To cook what food I have been able to procure."

Zeno sniffed the air. "Fish?"

"Aye."

"Very good."

They would need their energy. As soon as he was physically able, he would ascertain where they were. And from there continue on their way. His destiny would not be denied!

***

For two days they came across nothing. Not so much as a pelican, let alone a port.

Just two days ago an overabundance of water had almost killed them. And now the lack of it was threatening to do the same thing. The irony was not lost on Xanthe.

At first she thought that she was seeing nothing more than the glimmering of the sun off of the sea. But then, as she kept looking, she realized that it was coming from the landward side.

Her pulse quickening, she stepped up the pace. That was not water—it was metal. And where there was metal, there were people.

Catching on to Xanthe's observation, the rest of the group followed her lead, their pace increasing as they closed the distance. Soon they were close enough to make out what they were racing towards.

Spears. And holding those spears: People.

Aye, people. But not any people that Xanthe was familiar with.

Their bodies, curiously lacking hair, were as brown as baked clay. Lean and fit, they wore little more than a skirt that came to their knees, and some sandals. Their upper bodies were bare, save for ornaments and trinkets worn on their arms and wrists and necks.

What was more, they seemed to be wearing wigs upon their heads, rather than natural hair, shifting them as they sought relief from the sun's rays.

But by far the strangest thing had to be their mode of conveyance. For amid their camp there were no less than five horses, and harnessed to each, some kind of mobile stand with wheels.

"Chariots," Glauce whispered.

Xanthe eagerly took in the sleek lines and contours. To the Greeks this was cutting edge technology, a thing heard of, but never seen with one's own eyes.

As a warrior, she immediately appreciated the device as a means of waging war. Upon an open plain it would be unstoppable.

The men (about a dozen or so in all) began speaking to them in a tongue the Amazon did not recognize.

Glauce seemed to be concentrating, trying to cipher out what they were saying, while Heracles looked uncharacteristically pensive.

"They are Egyptians." The rhapsode seemed both stunned and smug. "We are in Egypt."

Egypt? That storm had thrown them hundreds of schoinos away.

"At least we are on the right continent." Iochier said, looking on the bright side.

"What say they?"

Glauce shook her head. "I know not. At best I can make out the odd word. There has not been much call to learn their language."

"They demand to know who we are."

The companions looked to the demigod. Would wonders never cease?

"You speak their language?"

"I have passed through these lands before. Though when I left, it was not on the most friendly of terms…"

"Go on."

"It was nothing, really," Heracles relayed. "Just a misunderstanding between myself and Busiris."

"Busiris?"

The Scion of Olympus began to closely inspect his footwear as a massive arm scratched the back of his head.

"Their king."

"And what was the nature of this 'misunderstanding'?"

"He wanted something that I was not prepared to give."

"Such as?"

"My life. So, rather than that, I took something from *him* instead."

"Such as?"

"*His* life."

"You killed the King of Egypt?" Glauce blurted out, wide eyed.

"He was not a very good king…"

Suddenly, the Egyptians fell silent as one pushed his way to the front. Taller than the others, he bore a more regal air.

Handsome in a cruel way, firm of limb and with a stride that denoted that he did not merely live in this world, but that owned it. Clad much the same as his countrymen, there was one feature that made him stand apart: instead of a wig, he wore a striped head covering, giving him more than a passing resemblance to a cobra.

Eying the company of foreigners coolly, he started to converse with them in heavily accented Greek.

"You are strangers. For what purpose are you in my land?"

"His land?" Iochier muttered. "Does he own this beach?"

"Aye, this beach and all others," the man remarked.

Iochier sought to avoid Glauce's murderous look.

"Know that you are in Egypt," the man continued. "And I *am* Egypt. As she thrives, I thrive. As she wars, I war. As she hurts, I hurt. We are one and the same. As the sun, the moon, the stars above, we are ever lasting, imperishable.

"I am Ramses, ruler of Upper and Lower Egypt. Man. King. God."

As immobile as a statue, he stood with his fists on his waist. And in that moment, with the sun at his back, casting his long shadow over the sand, he almost seemed to be that which he claimed to be. A god.

"And now, I demand to know who you are, and by what means have you come to my land unbidden?"

Xanthe was put off by the man's arrogance (how many self styled 'gods' were there, anyway?), but felt it prudent to swallow her misgivings.

Heracles took it upon himself to answer.

"We are but poor wayfarers tossed upon your shores by the fickle whims of the wind. That it should be Egypt that we are in fills us with awe and wonder."

"Your tongue would seem as honeyed as ever… Heracles."

There it was. The demigod's face darkened.

"Aye, you are known. Your size. Your bearing. Your great war club. There cannot be more than one such man in all the world. You are remembered well. You are remembered for having slain Busiris. Remembered—and thanked."

A smile broke out on the ruler's face. It seemed as foreign there as the Greeks were to Egypt.

"Busiris was an upstart who dared claim himself 'king'. The line of rulers of this land has been unbroken since the time of Menmes. That he felt himself worthy of the crown…" he laughed, his eyes cold even in mirth. "You did the throne a great favor the day you did kill that pretender. It did save Egypt from civil war. Never a good thing, and all the more so when there are other, outside, enemies to contend with.

"Nay, Heracles, Egypt is indebted to you. And as Egypt owes, so do I owe. How may I be of aid?"

"We need transportation," Xanthe interjected.

The king's men spoke up, outraged that a mere woman should address such an august personage. Ramses raised his hand, silencing them.

"You are ignorant of our ways," he told the travelers, "here, women are to be seen, not heard."

"As your Majesty said, we are strangers." The woman warrior's eyes never left his.

The tableau held for some seconds, until Ramses unleashed a laugh.

"I shall enjoy hearing more of you and your land. Women who carry arms, and demigods who travel with them. Let us retire anon." Turning away, he clearly expected them to follow.

"We have not time for this!" Xanthe hissed to Heracles.

"We also have no supplies. I know not about you, but my stomach rumbles with hunger."

"And what of Zeno? He hungers as well, yet not for food."

The demigod shrugged. "Perhaps he perished in the storm,"

"Would not Athena have notified us of such?"

"Fair enough. If he did survive, no doubt he was at least blown as far off course as we, perhaps he is even now, like ourselves, a stranger in a strange land. Besides," he added, rubbing his middle, "it has been some time since I have enjoyed royal hospitality."

***

The Great Nile River proved a sight to behold. Its length was truly staggering, as was the delta into which it emptied. Had Glauce not been sick the entire way, she would have doubtless remarked upon its beauty and power. The stark difference between the land directly abutting the river and that not more than a hundred steps distant was like night and day. The former lush, green, fertile. The latter, a sheer desert as far as the eye could see.

And while its wonders were not lost upon Xanthe, she would have soon soured of them. It was only Heracles' insistence that their direction happened to be carrying them closer to the Grove of Hera that held the Amazon's ire in check.

As the days rolled by, the blond battler found much time on her hands to take stock of their benefactor.

Ramses claimed not only lordship over his people, but their worship as well. If Zeno sought to be a god, Ramses felt that he already was one.

Only, he was not.

In a quiet moment, Heracles revealed that there was not a trace of divinity about the man. As he told it, one of godly blood could tell another, and Ramses was no more a god than the man who mucked out the royal stables.

Yet he acted the part, issuing orders as though from on high. And in truth, from a worldly perspective, he held more power than any one man in Greece, that country being broken up into many city-states, whereas in Egypt all pulled to the yoke of the same master.

When they had broken their fast, Ramses had explained that he had decided upon a hunting trip at the last moment, and thus it was this haste that should excuse his poor showing of retinue, he said by way of apology.

'Poor showing', he had said. It turned out that his entire troop numbered no less than four barges, each filled with people and animals. Cats, dogs, even pet jackals resided among no less than two hundred individuals. Soldiers and courtesans were accounted among their number, but the overwhelming majority were slaves brought along to administer to the needs of their masters.

Slavery was not unknown to Xanthe, it was common enough in Greece, but her fierce Amazonian spirit rebelled at the concept. Her people were all about living, and yes dying, free, on their own terms. The holding of people in bondage was a greater sin than even murder. At least the dead had a measure of peace.

Heracles was of the same opinion, having himself been a slave for a time. So it was that the sun drenched shores of the Nile seemed a mite darker to them.

The river itself teemed with life. Crocodiles, strange giant pigs (their guests told them they were called 'Hippopotamus'). All manner of livestock slaked their thirst by its current, their owners' farms conspicuous in their close proximity to the banks of the life giving thread.

The days passed as slowly as the hippos in the water, or at least that was the way it seemed to Xanthe. She chafed at the inaction. But Heracles told her that as they were traveling in the proper direction, it was better to do so 'in style' rather than trudge their own way. While she bowed to the logic, she did not have to like it.

Ramses appeared from below, leaping to the bow of the barge. One foot on the decorative figurehead, his arms spread wide. It seemed as though he were claiming the entire world as his own.

"Behold," he said, his voice rising. "Behold, Hundred Gated Thebes!"

Just then the barge turned a bend and the glory of the capital of the most influential empire on the face of the earth was revealed.

Xanthe was taken aback by the city's splendor, for even at a distance the place radiated power and strength.

White stone gleamed in the harsh sunlight, the temples and obelisks magnifying that orb's rays into a brilliance that pained the eye.

And then there were the people. Everywhere, people. The women as painted as a picture—even the men wore makeup.

The sounds, the smells, all of it washed out over the visiting Greeks, they whose country considered all other peoples to be barbarians. Here, *they* were the barbarians.

"A sight fit to rival the gates of Olympus itself," Xanthe heard Heracles say.

But she herself had only to look over at the oarsmen, chained to their posts, to be reminded that for all the shining achievements of Olympus, there is, at the back of it, a dark Tartarus.

CHAPTER 14

Zeno was still weak, yet he had insisted that they go. So it was that master and servant wandered out into the countryside.

It was not half a day before they were stumbled upon by a local patrol.

Being in no shape to either flee or fight, the duo quickly gave themselves up, and were just as quickly hustled about on a pre-determined course.

"Do you recognize them, Master?" Trepat asked as they marched.

"I have suspicions, nothing more. Their language does smack of Tyre—I heard it often enough at the royal court of Troy."

"Troy? Surely we were not thrown so far off course!"

"Nay, the Trojans use not outlanders to patrol their shores. Nor have we landed at Tyre itself, for we are not on an island."

"Then where are we?"

"More important Trepat, where are we going?"

That answer came as soon as they crested a rise. None could fail to divine their destination.

"Behold brothers!" one of the guard's yelled at the sight, "The Shining City of Carthage!"

***

The city was a beehive of activity. People were coming and going; some at the same time. Donkeys brayed, peddlers hawked their wares, children laughed, all was sound and motion.

Thebes made Athens look like a backwater Ionian village.

Glauce could not soak in enough of it, her head seemed as if it were on a swivel. To the rhapsode, this was paradise.

"Everyone and everything in such a frenzy. I have never seen anything like it!"

"It brings to mind the evacuation of Joppa before the coming of the Kraken…" Xanthe replied sedately.

"An evacuation be not far off the mark," Ramses answered. "You have come at a propitious time. Egypt has a new Pharaoh, a new start. As such, it deserves a new capital. All that which is needful for the administration of the empire is being moved. And as goes the government, so follows the commerce. All are in the process of transport."

"What be this new capital's name?"

"Pi-Ramesses!"

Iochier leaned into Glauce. "Not much of an ego with that one…"

"You shall attend a feast in your honor," the Pharaoh commanded, rather than requested. "We shall speak more of our two lands…"

"We can give naught but thanks to your Majesty for your generous offer, which we of course accept," Heracles responded in a statesmen like manner, in the process giving Xanthe a meaningful look.

In due course the demigod dropped back and allowed the Amazon to take him by the arm.

"What do you mean?" she demanded. "We waste time here."

"Look about, fair Xanthe. Do you truly think that we might leave when we wish? It is clear that Ramses is leery of outsiders; surely you have noted that we have been under guard our entire voyage. At this moment we are in fact more honored prisoners than actual guests."

The look on the Amazon's face was dark, but she nodded. "Aye, I have noticed their eyes always on us. What do you think he plans to do?"

The demigod shrugged. "More like as not to ply us for information as to our true intent. For all of its splendor, Egypt has had rough times as of late. Thus they are paranoid. Civil strife, foreign incursions, all have taken their toll on its collective psyche. As long as Ramses distrusts our intent, we shall not be allowed to leave his 'hospitality'."

"How can we convince him of our aims without revealing our quest?"

"We can not."

"That is not acceptable,"

Heracles chuckled. Leave it to an Amazon to be a master of understatement.

"Our best option is to wait for the time to part ways with his eminence without his knowledge. For I do not like the odds of wading through Egypt's armies in order to escape her borders."

Xanthe raised an eyebrow. "The mighty Heracles admitting that he be mortal?"

The demigod grinned. "Half mortal at any rate."

***

So, they were strangers in a strange land as well. It made sense.

As Zeno was led down the wide thoroughfare, past the fragrant shops and well kept homes, he noted how new everything was. How fresh the frescos were. How even the flagstones upon which he tread looked uncracked with age.

This city had not long been founded, these people not long here. A colony of extirpates founded on a forgotten corner of Africa.

Yet, what they lacked in roots, they more than made up for in zeal. The sheer effort that it must have required to carve a city of this size out of a hostile, foreign land…

"Where are we to be taken?" he asked their captors. "So that our benignity may be vouchsafed."

"All foreigners are to be vetted by her Majesty, the Queen. She shall decide as to what becomes of you."

A woman. It seemed to be a reoccurring theme in Zeno's life as of late.

***

The 'guest quarters' they found themselves in were larger than many a temple of Zeus. As was the statuary, all bearing the same likeness. That of Ramses.

Xanthe chaffed at being a 'not quite' prisoner. There were feasts in their honor, and they had the run of Thebes during the day as befit a visiting dignitary. But at all times she was reminded that they could not truly leave. The ever present guards made that clear.

"For your own safety," they had been assured.

However, not all of her companions shared her concerns.

Glauce had been too immersed in her access to the arts and knowledge of the great land to give much thought to anything else. Her inner rhapsode was in overdrive at the moment.

And as for Iochier, he currently lounged on one of the cushion-covered benches that were strewn about, allowing the newly entered, and scantly clad, slave girls (provided by Ramses to serve them) to feed him by hand.

Some innate sense causing her to glance up from her papyrus, Glauce's lips formed a thin line of disapproval at what she saw.

"Iochier! Are not these poor wretches lives not made miserable enough by being slaves? Would you add to their burdens? By using them as such you but continue to keep them down! You are free, would that all might share your good fortune!"

The young man frowned, chastised.

Glauce addressed one of the slaves directly.

"We thank ye. You may go now."

"Nay, good lady, I pray thee, nay," the slave answered, her dark eyes pleading. "Should we be sent away, it would be seen as displeasure on your part towards us, and we should be sorely punished."

The rhapsode was taken aback. "You speak Greek?"

"Aye," the slave girl nodded, "From a former master; in secret I did watch him. Watched and learned." Then, in a whisper, "I can read as well."

"What be your name?"

"Josanna," she answered, hesitantly.

"Josanna." Glauce's tongue wrestled with the strange name. "It does not have the sound of Egyptian."

"It is not. I am not Egyptian, but rather, Hebrew."

"Hebrew?"

"The name of my people."

The unfamiliarity of it only furthered to wet the rhapsode's insatiable appetite to learn.

"I have never heard of your people. Where is your homeland?"

Josanna's eyes were downcast. "We have no homeland. We are slaves in a foreign land. For centuries we have endured the lash, done as was decreed; died as was commanded."

Her eyes came up again, but now they held an inner fire, alight with that approaching fervor. "Yet it shall not always be so. Freedom shall be ours at long last."

"Has your Pharaoh promised you freedom?"

Josanna spat at the floor.

" 'Pharaoh'. Bah! Nay, it is God that has promised it. It be He whom have promised my people. We shall be free, and forever leave behind the sands of this accursed place."

Glauce's confusion showed.

"Which god?"

"I speak of the One True God, the maker of all. The Divine King of the Universe."

"What—what is the name of this god of yours?"

"What name does the sky go by? Or the water? God is that which is. Your false gods seek to glorify themselves at your expense. Pharaoh, Ra, Zeus, they all be lesser men, lesser beings, desperately in need of validation of themselves."

Again the Hebrew spat on the marble floor. The sound magnified as the room had gone silent.

Glauce was astonished. It was the very thing that Heracles espoused, and yet here they were in a far-flung land. Once more the idea of a higher power than that of the gods she had been reared to revere since she was but a mere slip of a girl.

The idea was intoxicating, the rhapsode's inner muse fairly sang with desire to learn more about both the idea and these strange enslaved people who hung on so doggedly to it.

"Will you tell more of such things? Of your ways, and your people?"

Josanna seemed to finally remember her station, and again looked scared. Glauce squeezed her hand.

"Please. I find your plight touching, and your ways of interest. It is my profession to know of the ways of the world, and those whom inhabit it. I would learn more of you and yours. Would you tell more of these things?"

Finally, slowly, the slave nodded.

***

The throne room was no less impressive than the rest of the palace, or for that matter, the city.

Columns lined the space, as thick around as a grown man. White marble, they extended to the upper reaches of the roof, providing both security and aesthetics. One could not help but feel small in their presence.

A wide walkway took up the space in between the stone rows. Covered in rugs, dyed the deepest of purples, it lead to the raised dais that held the royal throne of Carthage.

Wrought in gold and ivory, it reflected the light from the window behind, dazzling the eye of those that beheld it, further adding to the feeling of intimidation it was meant to convey.

And there, seated upon it, every bit as regal as her surroundings, was the monarch herself, Queen of Carthage.

The diaphanous gown's color was that of the sea itself by which the city stood. Its fabric clung to her shapely figure not unlike the tapestries that hung about the walls; tasteful, concealing, while at the same time revealing the beauteous structure over which it was draped.

Her skin looked to have been kissed by Apollo himself. Not brown, but neither alabaster. A rich blending of the two, a nexus where the genes of the East meet those of the West.

And upon those exposed shoulders rested a magnificent trestle of hair. Hair dark as midnight, and twice as long. Flowing, vibrant, it reflected its owner perfectly.

And to top it off, a large silver diadem, a crown fit for a queen. The center of which held an unblemished diamond. Flawless, perfect, its cold beauty seemed to enhance that of its wearer.

"Kneel." one of the attendants said, "Kneel before Queen Elissa of Carthage!"

CHAPTER 15

The Queen's expression betrayed none of her thoughts. Her eyes darted over Zeno and Trepat.

"What do we have here?"

"Foreigners, Highness," her royal steward replied. "They may be spies for our enemies. Hired mercenaries."

Queen Elissa continued to appraise the men, her cool demeanor giving the captives neither hope nor fear. At last she spoke.

"I think not. That *we* are foreigners is the contention our neighbors have with us, thus it seems unlikely that they would use foreigners to do their bidding.

"What have you to say on your own behalf?" she inquired of the prisoners.

"Great Highness," Zeno addressed from bended knee, "if I may be permitted to stand?"

At a gesture he arose, straightening his tunic.

"I am known as Zeno. This is my servant, Trepat. We are strangers in this land, yet even from afar, Carthage is spoken of in awe. A shining city by the sea. A city unmatched. A city unparalleled. A city under siege." He let that last part hang in the air.

"It was for this reason that we came, and it was for this reason that we were cruelly set upon by your enemies. It was my intention to come to you with an offer of help, to aid you. Two hundred hardened Greek warriors were at my back, ready to join you in your struggle for survival in this hard land."

Now his face took on a mournful cast, the very picture of despair.

"Yet we did meet with ill fortune. The winds, they came upon us while at sea and did dash our ships upon the shore, sending many a fine man to a watery grave. And yet, even as the survivors gathered what we could from the wreckage, we were set upon by the very foes we came to fight.

"Undermanned, fatigued, and caught unawares, we proved no equal match, though we acquitted ourselves as best we could under the circumstances. In the end there were but a handful of us left, thus we decided to make a final, fateful, charge. 'For Greece, for Carthage!' we shouted.

"Shoulder to shoulder we fought, giving our last measure of defense on these foreign shores, proving that Greek courage is not a myth.

"Only I and Trepat managed to break through. Wounded, lost, hunted, we did wander until your soldiers happened upon us. I regret that we have but our poor meager selves to offer to you. Yet what we have to offer, we do so as ardently now as when we first set out upon this voyage,"

Finishing with the artifice, he bowed his head humbly. Even Trepat, who had become used to his master's ways, found it hard to hold himself in check. Truly the man possessed the tongue of Hermes.

Queen Elissa gave him a long look. "It would be ungracious to turn away one who has come through so much to aid those who are not his own."

The Queen clapped her hands, and from opposite sides of the room, serfs came bearing trays of meat and drink, fruits and sweetbreads, and all manner of foodstuffs.

"Come, let us sup and speak more."

Even as the situation seemed to turn in his favor, Zeno was withdrawn. It was clear that it would be some time before he could manage to find his way free of this place. And what was more, he had need to find his Thunderbolts before he left. They were the key to everything. He praised himself for having thought of covering them up amongst his other goods. Goods that now resided who-knew-where within this city's walls.

Yes, this was going to take both time and charm. Fortunately for him, he possessed both.

***

Xanthe leaned against the lintel, looking at the hustle and bustle of the street.

Ramses had not been in jest. All day and all night the citizens of Thebes were in the process of moving.

Rich merchants with caravans of spices. Scribes with piles of parchment in their arms. Even poor beggars trying to latch onto a traveling party. All in preparation for a new capital. Everyone was on his or her way. Everyone except for Xanthe and her companions.

She liked nothing about this place. Not the sand that got everywhere. Not the inability to hold a conversation with anyone. Not even the Pharaoh himself, whom the Amazon found prideful and vain. Traits that would doubtless lead his people to trouble someday.

So it was with a face as stony as the wall against which she leaned that she cast a jaundiced eye over the scene.

"You had best move," Heracles said from behind, coming up to her. "Else someone might mistake you for one of the statuary."

"No fear of that," she snorted. "I do not resemble Ramses in the slightest."

The demigod laughed.

Though he had been on the throne but a short time, and though it was soon to no longer be the seat of government, Thebes was positively decorated with Ramses' image.

Painted on walls, carved into steps, etched onto jewelry, he was everywhere. Like the godhood to which he claimed, he was everywhere at once.

"How much longer must we endure his 'hospitality'? Time is wasting!"

"There can be no telling, though he will have to make his way to his new capital soon enough."

"Not soon enough as far as I am concerned."

"Not everyone shares your disdain for our sojourn here. Indeed, young Iochier and Glauce seem to have found means to entertaining themselves."

"A rhapsode can find solace anywhere there is pen and parchment. And as for Iochier…"

Once again the demigod's laugh boomed in the early morning air.

"Amazons are not known for our patience. And mine grows short."

***

As the days wore on, Zeno sought to ingratiate himself with the Queen more and more. He could not leave without his Thunderbolts. And he could not get near them on his own.

As best as he could ascertain, his personal belongings were being kept somewhere in the palace itself, locked away, his hosts knowing nothing of their value.

That is where Her Majesty came in.

Being the ultimate authority in the city, what she said went. Thus it was imperative to get on her good side. Thus began the wooing of the Queen.

At first it was pretences in discussing strategy. His observations as a visiting Greek 'General'. How he might aid Carthage in its struggle, etc.

Over time his presence was accepted, and thus he began to spend more one-on-one time with the Queen. Consequently, their meetings became increasingly informal.

Soon, the indoors were left entirely, and the two strolled the palace grounds speaking of military matters less and less, their conversations turning instead to philosophy.

The more they spoke to one another, the more the young Queen came to confide in this handsome stranger. So unlike her own people. As their Queen, she could see them only as dependents, not suitors. She was like a mother, and they, her children.

But Zeno, he was not one of her brood. He was far from her world and its strictures, filling a void in Elissa's life that she had not been aware existed.

So it came to be that one day found the two of them sitting amidst the royal garden, the foliage's greenery mirroring the vitality of the city itself.

Zeno kneeled, studying a plant. "It would seem that all is in fresh bloom. Your flowers, your city, yourself…"

Though used to compliments, a blush still tinged the Queen's cheeks, adding color to her already dusky features.

"I would know more as to how alike the great cities of the Greeks are to our own. Truly, how possible might an alliance be with them?"

"You are wise to consider an alliance with my people. For they are unmatched in all the world in either military prowess or learning."

The Queen sat heavily upon a bench; her head drooped, as though the weight of its crown were at times too much to bear.

"We have to spend our time defending ourselves from rude tribes that would see us thrown out of this new land. But it will not always be thus, there shall come a day when we are strong enough, secure enough in our place that we can look to the outside world. And when that day comes, Carthage shall be a force to be reckoned with!"

The Queen's eyes glittered as she envisioned the future of her people.

"And when that day comes, we shall have need of trading partners and the like. If Carthage is to make itself civilized, then it must associate with the civilized."

"Your situation is a prime one, not unlike that of Troy. By virtue of geographic position, they control most of the trade to and from Asia. And they too have only to contend with 'rude tribesmen', easily cowered by Troy's prominence gleaned from its mastery of the surrounding seas. Carthage could easily be the Troy of Africa."

"You do spin an enchanting picture."

Zeno bowed. "I seek only to give you good council, oh Highness."

She nodded regally, a smile playing at her lips.

"Come, I would hear more of the advantages of allying oneself with the Greeks…"

***

"—four hundred years. That is how long they have been in bondage in this country!"

Secluded in their plush quarters, Heracles laid out amongst the soft pillows while Xanthe stood rigidly at attention. But both listened to Glauce as she told them of what she had learned from the slave, Josanna. Even Iochier, who had been privy to the conversations, still stood rapt.

"It would seem that these Hebrew bear Ramses no good will."

"Indeed, they do not. They only wait until the day of their deliverance. What is more, they are not shy about letting the Egyptians know it!"

"They allow the slaves this hope?" Xanthe asked, intrigued.

"Aye," the rhapsode was getting more excited as she spoke. "They are always on the lookout for this 'Deliverer' the Hebrew speak of. It would appear that the idea of their slaves rebelling is never far from their mind."

"It would have to be a mighty man to free an entire people from the grips of this empire." Heracles mused.

"A Herculean task, one might say," Xanthe deadpanned.

A broad smile broke out on the demigod's face.

"A quip? From an Amazon? Will wonders never cease?"

***

The man's head was as bald as an egg. So freshly shaven that the Pharaoh could see his own reflection in it.

"You have a report?"

"Aye, Lord of Light, Father of the Nile, King of the World."

"Tell your Pharaoh what you have learned."

"My informants say that your guests have been in deep conversation with the slaves. The rumor of their Deliverer has been bandied about amongst them."

Ramses was a man driven by fear. Fear of losing the power and prestige of his forefathers. Fear of being the Pharaoh on whose watch the empire fell. And this fear drove his self-aggrandizement; and his paranoia.

Anything might threaten his reign, and thereby his, and Egypt's, ever lasting glory.

Once before, fear of a slave revolt had sent his predecessors to the extreme of executing the slaves' young, in the hopes of cowering them into their proper place. Yet still they longed for freedom.

More and more this talk of a Deliverer came, and more and more Ramses feared it, as he had feared nothing else before. If he was the head of Egypt, then the slaves were the backbone. And without them...

This talk of the coming of the Deliverer and now the coming of the Greeks... Did not Heracles already slay one would-be ruler of Egypt? Was it not well known that he had himself once been a slave, and hated the institution?

Who better to challenge the god-king of Egypt than a demigod?

"Your Pharaoh thanks you."

"I live to serve," the eunuch stated, groveling in the dust before his majesty's feet.

But Ramses had already forgotten the man's presence. There were matters of much more import upon his mind.

CHAPTER 16

It is lonely at the top. This, Queen Elissa knew. As did Zeno. And it was this knowledge that gave him the advantage he needed to worm his way into her affections.

From stranger, to confidant, to lover; all in a short amount of time. He had both the Queen's heart and her city laid at his feet. But the only thing that he wanted lay in the royal armory.

His Thunderbolts.

Why settle for a kingdom when he could have the world?

Zeno eased himself from the sleeping Queen's bed, careful not to wake her. Rising, he quickly dressed and set his plan into motion.

It was night, and the stars could been seen in a cloudless sky. The city reposed in slumber after a most hearty feast. A feast suggested by none other than Zeno himself. Knowing that the citizenry would be sound asleep after such a revel, he also knew that it would allow him to move about the city unnoticed.

Upon arriving at the royal armory, he boldly strode up to the lone guard on duty, who was more groggy than not.

"I am on a mission for her Highness, the Queen," the demigod addressed the man, conveying the weight of his words with a supercilious stare.

"W-what?" the guard asked, unsteady on his feet.

"It is the Queen's express wish that I attend to a matter of grave importance. In there." He nodded at the armory.

Zeno's face had become well known to the citizens of the city in the short amount of time he had been there. And what was more, his 'special' relationship with the Queen was also well known. As drunk as he was, the guard had enough wits about him to not get on the wrong side of the Queen's paramour.

The door closing behind him, Zeno let out a sigh of relief. Now to find what he was looking for.

It did not take him long to do just that. Thrown in a corner unceremoniously, sitting on the floor still in their urn, were the Thunderbolts.

Zeno luxuriated in their feel, letting their power fill him. It was time to leave this place.

But first, he needed a handier way to carry them. Scrounging amongst the armaments, he traded out the urn for a simple quiver.

"Guard!" he called as he lifted a nearby mace from a rack.

The guard never saw it coming.

Trepat met him at the prearranged location with both mounts and enough supplies to see them on their way. All that remained was to effect their escape from the city, made all the easier by the lax guard post-feast.

As quiet as the night itself, the two foreigners lifted the great wooden beam that served as the lock on the gate of Carthage.

Then, without a care as to the safety of the inhabitants of that great city, Zeno set off into the wilds with his servant in tow.

***

The Queen's anger had been a sight to behold. When she had found out that Zeno had fled, whilst leaving the city unprotected through the long night, her wrath had struck dread into the hearts of all of her subjects.

Pride warred with heartbreak as Queen Elissa looked out from the balcony of her quarters. The placidness of the tranquil sea acted as a counterbalance to the turbidity of her own mind.

That she, the ruler of Carthage, was so fooled was a grievous blow to her judgment. The matter made her look as foolish as a fishmonger's wife before her subjects. The loss of respect could mean the loss of the throne. Such things could not be taken lightly.

What was more, she was angry with herself for having fallen for the dark haired stranger. His 'otherness' served as a lure, feeding into her own sense of isolation. She had given her heart, her city, to him. That she had shared her bed with one who had not cared for her… She felt used, rejected.

Hugging her nude form, she cried out in frustration.

"A pox upon you and your kind! Enemies of Greece I now account my friends! Oh, beware Greeks bearing gifts of advice and council! If ever one of your foes makes his way to our shore, I shall treat him as the king you might have been!"

Alone with her tears, she stood gazing out towards the endless horizon.

***

It came in the dead of night.

The doors burst open, and torches were waved about as the Pharaoh's men hustled in.

Upstairs, in one of the larger sitting rooms, the companions heard the commotion. So it was that Ramses men did not find them unawares.

And there, at their head, hands on his hips, elaborate headdress in place, stood Ramses, Pharaoh of Egypt.

It was a grim assemblage indeed that met the royal 'visitors' as they entered the room.

Heracles folded his arms. "I take it this is not a social call?"

Ramses was not one to bandy words.

"You would have done better to stay out of Egypt, Son of Zeus. The Hebrew stay; they shall not be taken by any man, even if he be a demigod!"

Before the accused could utter his own defense, the royal troop was upon them.

Xanthe's frustrations at being held in captivity, her disgust for the Pharaoh, and her resentment at being attacked, all boiled over.

Twisting her body about, she caused a spearmen to miss his thrust. Instantly grabbing the weapon's shaft as it passed by, the blond battler yanked it from its owner's grasp, bringing the haft up to crash against his chin.

Even as he slumped to the ground, the Amazon was busy laying about with her newfound toy.

One hand swinging the spear, the other her sword, she was a whirlwind of death.

Beside her, Heracles had his hands full. Literally. In each he held an Egyptian by the throat, before knocking their heads together.

Glauce made her own way through the fracas, her cloak whipping behind with every twist and turn she made, even as the staff flashed ahead of her, issuing punishment to all in its way.

And then there was Iochier, who was engaged in a game of 'ring around the rosy' involving himself, a structural column, and one frazzled guard.

In all of the commotion no one paid any attention to the slaves.

Josanna kicked the shin of one of the guards. Yet even as he cried out, he was grabbed from behind by another slave, and soon was swarmed by them.

It was at this point that most men would have had misgivings about their plan of attack. But not Ramses, to him nothing was beyond his ability to control.

Sword drawn, and a curse upon his lips, the Pharaoh of Egypt pressed forward to carry the day himself.

His snarl was in direct opposition to Xanthe's smile. She noted his charge even as she eviscerated one of his men.

But before the lion and lioness could meet, the Pharaoh was restrained by his own troops, intent on getting him out of the way of all harm—even if it must be over his own objections.

Forming a human wedge, the stalwart men ushered their nearly apoplectic sovereign from the building, leaving behind their dead and wounded.

Xanthe's breast heaved, even as Heracles laid a restraining hand on her shoulder, checking her desire to give pursuit.

"Now might be a good time to make our goodbyes to this land."

"He is right."

Turning, they saw that it was the slave, Josanna, that spoke.

"You have dared to raise a hand to Pharaoh. Your lives are now forfeit."

"As are yours," Glauce answered, a pained look on her face. "By taking part on our behalves you have sealed your own doom."

Josanna waved her concern off. "As slaves we are worse than dead."

But the rhapsode persisted.

"We can not allow you to die on our account." She turned to Xanthe for confirmation.

"Worry not for us," the Hebrew insisted. "We shall not stay."

"What will you do? Where will you go?"

"North," the beauty replied. "To a promised land. Come with us, you will be welcome."

"Our path leads elsewhere," Xanthe replied.

"Very well. Yet, your coming has done us a great kindness, and for that we would do one for you."

"How so?"

"We shall cover your flight, leading the Pharaoh and his troops along our own trail, thus leaving yours unseen."

Glauce began to interject, but Josanna put a hand on her shoulder, smiling.

"It is settled. Come, we need to be away from here before the Pharaoh's men return."

Under a cloak of darkness, all was made in readiness.

"We leave you here," Xanthe told the Hebrew, trying to get a handle on her strange new mount. They called it a 'camel'.

The Jewess quickly hugged them each in turn, causing Iochier to blush not a little.

"Blessings be upon you."

"And you!" Glauce returned.

With a smile, and an upraised hand, the former slaves were off.

"Come." Heracles said, eying the streets. "Let us make our own departure. I find that I grow weary of this clime."

***

"They have fled, oh King."

The Pharaoh sat long on his throne, motionless. His eyes smoldered, taking on a far away cast.

The ruler of Upper and Lower Egypt appeared oblivious to the low murmur that ran through the lookers on, their comments hurriedly whispered behind upraised hands.

At last he spoke, his voice sounding remote, hollow.

"Their presence here never occurred. Their names are to be stricken from every record, every tongue. The very mentioning of them shall be death. History itself is to have no memory of their ever being here. Egypt shall not be embarrassed by foreign barbarians.

"So let it be written, so let it be done."

CHAPTER 17

The heat shimmered off of the vast endless dunes of sand. They had traded one ocean for another. Just as featureless, the grainy sea of brown continued on unbroken, heaving and sighing as it continuously shifted under its own weight.

One topped a crest only to see countless others all around, before once again going along one's way.

Up and down. Side to side. Would that they had a ship in which to ride these particular waves.

But instead of sea spray, it was sand that stung their faces as they slowly traversed.

"Just think Trepat, the Immortal Grove of Hera. And within, the Golden Apples of Immortality, the fruit from which is made Ambrosia, the Food of the Gods."

"Is it not dangerous, my liege?" Trepat asked, not for the first time.

"Aye, yet am *I* not dangerous?" Zeno smiled, rustling his quiver of Thunderbolts.

***

"Are you sure this is the way, Heracles?" Glauce asked dubiously, not for the first time.

"Aye. This stretch of sand looks familiar..."

"Familiar? It is sand; it all looks the same!" An edge had crept into the generally affable rhapsode's demeanor. The motion of her camel reminded her stomach unpleasantly of the rocking of a boat.

But it was true; to the naked eye all looked the same, regardless of where one happened to cast one's gaze. Once they had left the great river's bank, so too did they leave life as they knew it. To people used to mountains and trees, the stark lack of, well, *anything* was disconcerting.

"It is only a matter of time until we come across Atlas. And once he is sighted, then the grove can not be far beyond."

"Atlas," Glauce repeated, a trace of her former good cheer in her voice. "The once proud Titan sentenced to forever bear the weight of the heavens upon his back."

"And he was one of the lucky ones!" Heracles' laugh reverberated across the great sandy expanse.

***

The scenery had blurred into one great splotch of brown. Were it not for the bright blue of the sky, they might have forgotten that there was any other color in the world.

But finally, at long last, there it lay: far off on the horizon, a dark smudge, or line. But as they came closer, step by arduous step, the line grew darker, wider, more distinct.

Mountains. And it was there, within those mountains, that resided the next stop in Zeno's plan for universal domination.

It would be days more before they found themselves at the very foot of the earthen barrier—not to mention at the foot of something else entirely.

Namely, Atlas, the great Titan. As large as life he stood, his feet wider than the mightiest tree trunk, his body extending an incredible height, so much so that from a distance he blended into the mountains themselves.

Yet this was no mountain, but an immortal, covered in the grime of untold ages.

Stooped over, head hung low, his shoulders lost in the clouds upon which they held the Titan to his eternal service, a burden that was his alone to bear.

Trepat trembled in awe, his eyes wide, his mouth agape, too frightened to move, let alone think.

In truth, Zeno too felt the almost magnetic pull of the sight, though he hid it better.

Catching his breath, he addressed the Titan in preemptory tones, "Atlas, I seek an audience with you."

Nothing happened.

Peeved, the godling spoke again.

"Atlas, I would treat with you. So demands Zeno, Son of Zeus!"

A great sound rent the air, like that of stone scraping on stone. They could hear, as well as see, the massive eyelids of the Titan lift, and so gazed full on into his eyes, eyes that bespoke of time immemorial.

"Thou hast the temerity to speak thusly to one such as myself?" rumbled a voice like thunder. "I, who was old before the world was new? I, to whom thou art like a bug? Would that I had not my labor to perform, lest I would swat thee as the bothersome gnat that thou art, oh whelp of Zeus!"

Zeno drew himself up to his full height, as miserable an effect as it had.

"It would behoove you to treat such as I with respect; shortly I shall be your master!"

Atlas laughed, the reverberations of which felt as an earthquake to those below.

"As thou can see, mine master is none other than Zeus himself. By his decree I doth be tasked with holding up the heavens. Unceasing, unremitting, unto the ending of the world."

"Would you like to see Zeus serving in your stead?"

"Explain."

"You have but to answer a question and your freedom is assured. One answer and an eternity of labor shall be lifted, and in your place my hated Father!"

Though hard to tell, the stony face seemed intrigued.

Zeno pressed his advantage.

"Where is Hera's Grove of Immortality?"

***

The yawning distances required to traverse had taken their toll on some of the party. Hot and sore, it took all of Glauce and Iochier's effort just to cling to their perches.

Yet Xanthe and Heracles remained alert, heads erect, undaunted by the breakneck pace they had set for themselves.

Time had been of the essence; comfort had not. Now that they were under way again, Xanthe was ever more keen to push on, more and more worried that they would be too late—in contrast with Heracles' more prosaic posture.

"Thither from here?" the warrior woman assayed, taking in the foothills of the mountain range they had been riding towards all day.

"Let us find out."

Cupping his hands, the demigod called out, "What ho there!"

"Whom do you call?" Iochier asked through cracked lips. "There is no one about."

Ignoring him, Heracles continued to call out seemingly to no one. "What, no words for an old cohort?"

Then, to the great astonishment of everyone, save Heracles, there was a response. As though the earth itself spoke.

" 'Cohort', base swindler? Vile trickster! Thou art no friend of mine, spawn of Zeus!"

"The mountain—it lives!" Iochier gaped.

"It is no mountain, rather the Titan, Atlas," Glauce corrected, no less awed.

"Trickster?" Heracles tried to sound hurt. "Have you forgotten that it was *you* who tried to trick *me* into carrying *your* burden? Let bygones be bygones."

"I can guess what hast brought thee here again." Atlas responded, sullenly.

"Aye, we seek directions to Hera's Grove."

Xanthe's head whipped around.

"Directions?" she asked, accusingly. "I thought that you have been to the Grove before."

The Titan chuckled, and the ground heaved to and fro.

"Nay, it was I who retrieved the sacred fruit. Mayhap thou would like to take mine place whilst I go in thy stead again?" he asked, slyly.

The demigod guffawed.

"Nay, directions will suffice."

"Why should I tell thee anything? Thou art no friend of mine!"

"That is why you will tell us. For intruding upon Hera's most sacred grove will assuredly bring down her wrath. And what could please you more than that?"

Several moments passed, and all held their breath until finally the Titan spoke again. This time there was a hint of amusement in his voice, and Xanthe distrusted it.

"I shalt reveal to thee the secret path. I feel that thou doth deserve what awaits thee."

He commenced to tell them of the hidden byways which they must follow, and soon they were on their way.

"I like not his sudden helpfulness, even in spite," Xanthe confessed, glancing back at the towering figure. "He knows that you have managed to avoid Hera's wrath thus far."

"He does not feel that we shall return," Heracles explained. "He thinks us ignorant of the grove's inhabitants."

"Nymphs. So the legends say," Glauce filled in upon seeing Iochier's blank look.

"Aye, on occasion. Yet there is another, a guardian set in place to prevent those whom would seek entrance, lest mortal man attain immortality. For the gods set that aside for themselves."

"Guardian? Is not the Queen of the Gods guardian enough?" Iochier wondered aloud.

"Nay. Her Highness can not be expected to be there at all times—Father Zeus' wandering eye requires too much attention from her!"

Xanthe's serious expression was in direct opposition to the one of mirth on Heracles' face.

"Who is this guardian?" she asked.

The demigod waved his hands about airily.

"Naught but a great worm."

"It makes a certain amount of sense," Iochier mused. "Earthworms are known to inhabit gardens…"

Glauce rolled her eyes. "He means a dragon."

"A dragon?" the woebegone warrior squeaked, his eyes wide with fear.

"We have already faced sea serpents and mad tyrants, what have we to fear from an over large lizard?" Glauce piped up, trying hard to overcome her own feelings of misgiving.

"That is the spirit!" Heracles laughed.

***

"There it be Trepat, the Grove of Immortality." Zeno whispered as the two spied from the bushes.

Resplendent in look, and fragrant in smell, it was an oasis out of place in this hilly, arid, chain of mountains. As out of place as snow in the Underworld.

Perpetually in bloom, the flora bore all the colors of the natural world, and some not seen outside of this place.

Big, small, impossibly delicate, and infinitely ugly. The range was staggering. From redwoods to bluebells. From mosses to sunflowers that gleamed as though they were actual suns.

But there, in the very center of it all, stood the prize of the lot. That which had brought Zeno halfway across the known world.

The Tree of Immortality, from which hung the Golden Apples of Hera. The fruits by which the gods themselves retained their immorality.

And there, underneath the tree, lay the largest and most fearsome dragon in all the world: Landon, the Guardian of the Gods. It was to him that they entrusted the keeping of their most precious secret.

The dread beast stood watch, ever vigilant, never leaving the grove, at hand lest someone dared breach the sanctity of the place.

Curled around the tree like a monstrous scarf, the reptile's scaly sides heaved to and fro as it slept.

While snake-like, it differed from its minuscule cousins in that it had four legs besides. Ungainly, it elicited a feeling of revulsion from all whom gazed upon it.

Were he any other man, Zeno would have turned away at that moment and given up his foolhardy venture. But a madness most severe resided in this one, and such thoughts were not even allowed entrance into his mind.

His plan was simple. He would have Trepat lure Landon away from the tree, retrieve the fruit himself, and be on his way. If need be, he had the Thunderbolts to vouchsafe his life.

For his part, Trepat was not keen on the plan.

"Why do you not simply slay him outright, Master?" he had asked, more than a little concerned.

"He is too near the tree," had been the retort. "I would destroy it along with the dragon."

"Yet, if the beast should fall upon me…"

The servant found himself thrust out into the open, 'helped' on his way by Zeno.

Immediately, a great eye opened, the golden orb coming to rest upon the poor unfortunate Greek.

CHAPTER 18

"I would hear the plan once more," Iochier demanded, watching his footing on the rocky terrain.

"If we see Zeno, we kill him. If we do not, we wait." Xanthe's voice was as hard as the rocks they traipsed over.

"I think he meant the dragon." It was Glauce's turn to seek reassurance.

"We shall stay hidden in the brush," Heracles assured. "If there be no sign of Zeno, then there is no reason to show ourselves in the Grove proper until he arrives."

Heracles raised his hand, calling for a halt. Then, putting a finger to his lips, he made to part the bushes to scope out the Grove when a great roar rent the air, startling all of them.

Throwing caution to the wind, they looked out upon the Grove and were stunned by the scene before them.

A man raced for his life, fear lending him speed as he was chased by what could only be Landon; a behemoth, all gaping maw and obscene undulating girth, the very passing of which caused the ground to shake.

But perhaps even more arresting, there, away from the streaking figures, underneath a simple tree bearing golden fruit, stood Zeno.

He spied them as soon as they him. And though as surprised as they, it did not still him as he leapt to perform his task.

Breaking into a run, Xanthe sped towards the rogue godling, heedless of aught else. In her wake followed her companions.

Landon's head wheeled about, taking note of the new visitors. Raising his maw high, he let vent another earth shaking roar.

Seeing that the walking nightmare now make for them instead, Glauce yelled, "Scatter!"

Which she and Iochier did. Heracles, however, held his ground, a smile wreathing his broad whiskered face. Bringing his great war club to the fore, he baited the approaching monstrosity.

"Pay heed, friend Glauce, you shall have quite a tale to tell once this day is done!"

As Heracles engaged the Creature of the Grove, Xanthe padded after Zeno.

So close! The godling fumed. A second more was all that he had needed! But now he had to worry about not only the dragon, but this wild Amazon and her playmates! How had they managed to live through what he had done to Mount Etna? It was not fair!

He could not leave without the fruit, but neither could he stay and be killed.

Running blindly through the thicket, he stumbled over an exposed tree root. Sprawling, he went tumbling down an incline, until finally coming to rest in a shallow brook.

Looking up, he saw Xanthe follow him down, only with more caution.

There was nothing else for it, he had to fight. At least until he could think of some way to salvage the situation.

Quickly rising, he drew his sword, heedless of the wet clothes that clung to him like a funeral shroud.

"There is more than enough fruit for all of us," he wheedled. "When I ascend to my cosmic throne there shall be a need for a new pantheon of gods. How does the title of 'Goddess of War' sound to your ears?"

"Hollow."

The Amazon stalked in slowly, her eyes never leaving Zeno.

"You could replace Athena herself!"

It was the wrong thing to say to an Amazon.

Without a rejoinder, Xanthe lunged, her sword seeking Zeno's lifeblood.

Jumping back, he swallowed a curse. Conversation was at an end.

As Xanthe pressed the attack, Zeno tried to find a way out. He parried rather than thrust. His sword work was purely defensive as he sought a way to flee.

As the two warriors battled, a fight of a decidedly different sort was taking place elsewhere.

Landon's massive jaws sought Heracles again and again. And again and again the demigod rolled away, causing the dragon frustration no end, even as the man himself was amused.

"Come now, is that the best you are capable of? Are you a dragon, or a 'drag on' Hera's good will?"

With a deafening roar, Landon struck out. But this time, instead of rolling away, the demigod side stepped, and then, legs firmly braced, swung with his prodigious might the war club in his hands, landing a titanic blow on the monster's exposed skull.

The dragon was rocked by the force of it, wobbling to one side before shaking his head clear.

"They say never play with a dragon, lest you be burned. They might say the same for he whom the dragon plays with!"

Meanwhile, trying her best to stay out of the rampaging beast's way, was Glauce. Though eager to help in some way, she knew that it was useless.

Yet even as she wondered about her own usefulness, Iochier's cry caught her ears.

"Zeno's servant! Over there!"

Sure enough, Trepat was trying to find a place of his own to hide.

"After him!" the rhapsode yelled above the tumult, as she and Iochier gave chase.

***

Zeno's two-handed slash came up short, as Xanthe's blade blocked it.

Slipping the two weapons loose, the Amazon clipped Zeno's chin with an elbow.

Smarting, the would-be-god broke away, trying to gain some distance.

But Xanthe pressed him at every turn. It was all that he could do to keep her at bay. He had yet to figure out a plan of escape, Xanthe's attacks coming too fast and too frequently.

Blocking a strike, Zeno instantly brought his keen edge back the way it had come, in hopes of decapitating his opponent.

But the Amazon was too fast. Ducking, she allowed Zeno's counterstrike to pass harmlessly over her head as she brought her own sword into play once more. This time in the hopes of spearing the godling like a fish.

In a panic, Zeno jumped back just in time, feeling the blade pierce his tunic even as he cleared the distance.

Growling, Xanthe advanced. Zeno was exasperated.

"When I become a god, I shall burn every Amazonian village I can find to the ground!"

Xanthe let her sword do her talking, and its blows rang out like a blacksmith at his forge.

This was not going well, Zeno thought. Not well at all.

***

Trepat saw them coming through the glade. Not having a plan, he simply ran blindly, hoping to lose them somewhere amidst the grove's bounty of flora.

But Glauce refused to let him out of her sight. Behind her was Iochier; just as keen, if not in as good of shape as the lean rhapsode.

A large flock of colorful birds, the type of which he had never seen, afforded Trepat the opportunity he was looking for. Disturbed by his passing, the fowl took to wing, obscuring his pursuers' vision momentarily.

Leaping into the overhanging branches of a nearby tree, he pulled himself up quickly and hid.

To Glauce and Iochier it was as if he had simply disappeared.

"Where is he?" Iochier asked, looking about, flabbergasted.

Glauce slammed a fist into her palm, frustration writ large on her delicate face.

***

Landon had brought his tail into action, lashing it about as if he were swatting at a fly. Which, from his perspective, Heracles might as well have been. Albeit a fly with a vicious 'bite'.

Heracles in turn now had to worry about both ends of the fiend. In a case such as this, offense was the best defense.

Utilizing his mighty leg muscles, he launched himself at the gargantuan beast, bringing his war club down upon the dragon's exposed flank.

Landon's frame shuddered, the sinew and bone quivering as it sought to absorb the impact of the godly blow.

A scream of pain escaped from the monster's muzzle as its head twisted around to snatch at the bothersome demigod.

Dropping his club, Heracles reached out as the cavernous mouth sought to close about him, and using all of his natural born strength, he grabbed the beast's jaws with his bare hands.

Therein a titanic battle ensued, Landon seeking to close his jaws and thus crush the one who dared attack him, and Heracles, for his part seeking to wrestle the creature down.

Like a typhoon, the great lizard rolled, flipped, flopped, and leapt in its attempts to dislodge Heracles' grip.

Trees uprooted, wildlife was sent scattering, and the air was filled with the din of combat.

And like the typhoon, everything in its path was affected. Everything, and everyone.

***

Xanthe could see that he was tiring.

His guard was getting sloppy. His cuts were not as crisp. And his thrusts were proving halfhearted at best.

The Amazon redoubled her efforts, sensing that the end was near.

A sense that Zeno shared.

He could not keep up this pace for much longer. Though it galled him to admit it, Xanthe was better than he. Her life had been steeped in the arts of war, for him it was more of a hobby. And that difference was beginning to tell.

But even as he racked his brains for a solution to his current problem, it came to him unbidden.

The first thing they heard was the noise, like the rushing of some great river. It was a 'wave' of destruction, but not one born of water. Rather, it was the sound of trees thicker around than a man's middle being snapped like kindling.

In horror, both looked up in time to see it: Landon, the dragon, rolling, thrashing, clawing; and there, in his very jaws, locked in mortal combat, Heracles.

It was the briefest of glimpses, and then the storm washed over them, and both felt that they were back out in the tossed waves of the deep blue ocean.

***

They heard the noise, but it did not provide enough warning.

Glauce and Iochier were taken unawares by the sheer speed of it all, like a tidal wave sweeping through.

One second the rhapsode had bent over looking for a trace as to Trepat's whereabouts, and the next, she, Iochier, and the very trees themselves, were torn from their roots and sent flying, as rag dolls before the coming of a broom.

***

Through the whole ordeal Heracles clung tenaciously to his perch. Bruised, battered, scratched and scarred, he refused to slacken his grip upon the monster. If he was to die this day, he would at least bring company with him.

The sky and ground blurred into one as the two rolled over and over through the grove, cutting a swath of destruction in their wake. The likes of which Hera would no doubt be displeased with.

***

All was still. No birds sang. No crickets chirped. Not a creature was stirring, not even a mouse. All that could be heard was the sound of the wind in the leaves.

Painfully, slowly, Xanthe's eyes opened upon this scene. Forcing herself up, she groaned.

Sore and aching, the Amazon felt more dead than alive. But alive she was.

Wincing at the pain in her neck, she took stock of her surroundings.

The grove was a shambles.

Downed trees were everywhere. A massive scar of broken vegetation gave mute testimony as to what had transpired.

And there, in the middle of all that devastation, the corpse of Landon.

Xanthe could see the white of the dragon's eyes as they stared off into eternity. But the most striking feature about it was its jaws: they hung loose, broken.

The Son of Zeus had done it. He had wrenched the dragon's jaws asunder, and in so doing, killed the beast. A feat that Xanthe would have thought impossible, even for a demigod.

But of the slayer, nothing was to be seen. Assaying the destruction, Xanthe slowly worked her way through what was left of the grove, a feeling of trepidation growing in her breast.

Upon sighting each new pile of debris, the Greek could not help but worry if one of her companions were beneath it. Or alternately, hope that her enemies were.

It was while passing one of these piles that a hand shot out and grabbed Xanthe by the leg.

She almost cleaved it in twain by instinct before realizing it for what it was. Bending down, she pulled its owner free.

The hand proved to belong to Iochier, who, to hear tell, got separated from Glauce after Landon's wave of devastation rolled over them.

Together, they searched for the others. Xanthe methodically, Iochier franticly.

Xanthe was about to check another spot when a cluster of broken foliage erupted into the air, and a wild roar went with it.

There, whole, if not a bit worse for wear, was Heracles. A smile, as always, plastered on his face.

"A tale indeed this will make! The day Heracles did slay the fell dragon Landon. Freeing the world of one more monster, and tweaking Hera's braids in the bargain!"

And though she made an effort to do so, the Amazon could not help but smile at the demigod.

"What of our friends, and brother Zeno?" he asked at last.

When informed of the unknown nature of both, he was once more the man of action. Though bloodied, he was not bowed.

"Come then! Let us find our little rhapsode, the sooner she is found, the sooner she can tell of these heroic deeds!"

"If she lives…"

But live she did, as Iochier was to find out the hard way.

It was while looking for her that he saw a branch that was not a branch. Upon further investigation, he noted that it was too straight, too smooth, that it was in fact no branch at all but rather a staff—Glauce's staff.

Digging through the brambles as fast as he could, he found the rhapsode's stiff form.

She was not breathing.

Panicking, Iochier did the only thing that he could think of.

Opening her mouth, he put his own to it and breathed for her. Expelling his own breath into her lungs.

At first nothing happened, then all at once her eyes flew open.

A single heartbeat passed, their two lips still pressed firmly together, their breath intermingling.

Then Glauce's hand came up and slapped Iochier. Hard.

Glauce's rescuer leapt to his feet, nursing his face.

"You were not breathing," he explained.

"Oh. I—I see. I thank you," Glauce stammered, blushing a deep crimson.

"I—I was not taking advantage—"

"Of—Of course not. I was... Surprised, is all." Her face reached a new level of red.

Both avoided eye contact as their mutual embarrassment grew until Xanthe and Heracles found them.

"Excellent!" Heracles clasped the two in a bear like embrace. "Now we have but to find Zeno."

A task which proved to be in vain, as no sign of him was to be found. Either dead or alive.

"It is fair to assume that brother Zeno has made off with what he came for.

"Doubtless in the ruckus he and his servant had managed to slip away, and in doing so procured some of the immortal fruits. Which could only mean one thing."

"He is on his way to the Underworld," Xanthe finished the train of thought. "All that remains is for him to free the Titans from their eternal prison."

"How does he intend to get there?" Iochier asked, puzzled.

"It is said that there are many different entrances throughout the world," Glauce informed, sitting upon a rock to ease her aching limbs. "Caves spread all about, deep and ancient."

"You are correct," Heracles confirmed. "I did use just such a one on occasion. Have you ever heard of the time I retrieved the three headed dog Cerberus from the very Gates of Hades?"

"Where is the nearest entrance?" Xanthe put in hastily, eying Glauce.

The rhapsode frowned prettily as she sought to dredge up the information from her mind.

"I have heard tell," she teased slowly, "that there lies an entrance on a group of islands not far from this Immortal Grove."

"To the seashore it is then."

But before Xanthe could start off, Heracles checked her.

"One moment. You have forgotten one necessary detail."

The Amazon looked askance.

"Yonder Tree of Immortality. You had better partake of its fruit prior to entering Hades' abode. That is of course assuming you wish to come back out alive."

The Amazon looked grave.

"You need not fear overstepping your bounds," the demigod commended. "Or have you forgotten that it is only through the constant consumption of the fruit that the gods remain ever young? Its effects shall wear off. Fear not, your mortality is safe."

"What of you?" Iochier asked the demigod, as he bit into the golden fruit. "Do you not need to also partake?"

Heracles smiled. "Nay. I have these to see me safely out of Hades' domain," he said, balling his massive hands into fists."

***

When Zeno had awakened, he had found everything in shambles. Of the Amazon and the others he saw nothing.

Instinctively, he checked his back: the Thunderbolts were still there.

Careful to pick his way through the aftermath, and mindful of his surroundings, he marveled at the Tree of Immortality, still upright after all that had transpired.

With its fruit he was now unstoppable.

Afterwards, it was but a nonce to find Trepat wandering dazed and confused.

"Come, enjoy the fruits of your master's labors."

And with that, Zeno led them from the grove.

"Where—where are we bound, Master?" Trepat asked, groggily.

"Our way lays beyond, towards the sea."

"We have no ship."

"We shall not need one."

CHAPTER 19

The foursome came out of the grove, making their way to the seashore.

Glauce's moan over the possibility of another ocean voyage died on her lips as she saw the scene that greeted them.

For there before them, littering the sand all up and down the shoreline, were feathers. Masses of feathers, as though every bird in the sky had molted at the same time.

And amongst those piles of feathers, dug into the beach's sand, was a large pit in which something bubbled.

Intrigued, Iochier got closer for a better look, only to recoil, holding his nose. His face held a look of disgust.

Xanthe took a deep breath, steeling herself against the pungent aroma.

"Renderings," she said. "Melted animal fat."

"That would explain the lack of birds amidst the presence of so much plumage." Glauce looked about, bewildered. "Yet, to what end?"

Xanthe noticed the smile that played at Heracles' lips.

"What be it?"

"Brother Zeno is a sly one," the demigod said, a chuckle threatening to erupt from his chest. "He has hit upon a way to cross the water, sans ship."

"How?"

"Fly."

"Fly?"

"Aye. He slew yon sea birds, melted them down for the fat to make wax out of, then used their feathers in order to make his own set of wings."

"Wax wings… As Daedalus made!" Glauce ejaculated.

"Aye. And as the wax is still hot, Zeno was here not long ago." Heracles cast his eyes towards the sky. "It is as good a way to transverse the distance as any other."

"You do not propose us to *fly*!" Iochier exclaimed, dreading the answer.

"*Anything* is preferable to sailing!" Glauce put in heatedly.

***

It all came together quickly. The raw materials were already at hand.

With that done, it was but a short trip back up into the mountains.

"Lift," Heracles explained. "The higher we start out, the better our chances of flying rather than falling."

"What now?" the rhapsode asked, apprehensive.

"Flap."

And with that, he shoved her off the ledge.

Glauce rocketed out in to the air, too startled to do anything.

Heracles cupped his hands about his mouth and yelled, "Flap! Flap your wings, little one!"

In a rush of panic she did just that—and not a moment too soon, for just then an upward draft caught her, and sent her soaring up into the wild blue yonder.

The rhapsode was mesmerized by the experience. Like a bird she flew, the air rushing through her hair, feeling the sensation of freedom that came with the severing of the bonds of gravity.

Heracles smiled as he watched her circle overhead. He turned to Iochier. "Now, your turn."

The Greek had taken on a shade nearly as green as the waters below. With the air of a condemned man, Iochier emitted a strangled cry as he ran and leapt off of the promontory.

Awkwardly, fearfully, he flapped his arms, and by extension the wings fastened to them. And though not pretty, it was enough to keep him aloft.

"Fair lady," Heracles bowed deeply to Xanthe.

Flexing her arms, the Amazon checked over her wings one final time.

Instinctively, she spread her arms out wide, like a gull, and with a stride as graceful as that of any swan, fell away from the cliff, only to pop back up a moment later on the winds.

Once Heracles joined them in the air, they wordlessly set out for the horizon.

***

The first thing Zeno did upon landing was to toss away his wings. Fixing his tunic, the godling strode boldly into the mouth of the gaping cavern that greeted him and Trepat upon their arrival to the island.

Dark as pitch, neither could see so much as the hand in front of their own face. Ominous, foreboding, it was as if they had entered a void from which there was no return.

The two walked on in silence until finally, strangely, they could see a light. And this seemed to scare Trepat more than the dark had. But as always, Zeno pressed on.

The light grew as the travelers went on, until it fully lit their way. And by this new strange illumination they could see a massive set of double doors set within an arch in the stone.

And before these doors stood the great hound Cerberus, each of his three heads projecting an attitude of extreme menace. As black as the gate he guarded, the massive mastiff's presence was a forbidding one.

Jaws gaping, drool pooling at his feet, the great dog growled a deep, throaty growl that echoed off of the rocky tunnel.

Smelling of sulfur and mildew, the gatekeeper of the Underworld looked at the two, but made no overt action.

Zeno casually strolled up to the beast.

"Fear not, Trepat, he has no power to prevent those from entering—only from leaving. And even in that, he is powerless against us. For we have partaken of the Fruit of Immortality, the effects of which shall more than see us through our little sojourn here."

Laughing, the demigod passed by, Trepat at his heels. Leaving Cerberus to look on threateningly.

All too easy, Zeno thought to himself.

***

"The final stop. In more ways than one," Heracles joked upon landing.

Before them loomed the mouth of a great cave, the inside of which looked to be as dark as the night sky.

"It is the way?" Xanthe wanted to know.

At Heracles' nod, she led the party into the inky blackness.

"Mayhap we should light a torch?" Glauce suggested.

"Nay, no natural light will take here. Wait, and one shall be provided for us."

True to his word, it soon began to grow lighter; but a strange, unnatural light. And it was then that they wished that it had remained dark.

"Large dog… Large dog…" Iochier stammered, his mouth suddenly having gone dry.

Upon hearing the newcomers, Cerberus growled. And when he laid eyes on Heracles, he went to pieces.

One of his heads began to bay; another turned away and whimpered, whilst the third snapped his teeth in both anger and frustration.

For his part, the demigod smiled.

"I see that you have not forgotten. I fear that I have not the time to play with you. If you are good, mayhap I shall bring back a haunch for you to feed on."

The party proceeded past the hound through the giant iron wrought gates he protected.

The way was silent, their footfalls echoing as they padded down a stone path of black ballast, darker than the gray walls that surrounded them.

"The Road of the Dead," Glauce murmured, her voice carrying all the same.

None spoke again until the sound of running water reached their ears. The sound was made all the louder by the utter silence which proceeded it.

The River Styx, the River of the Dead. The border between the Living and the Dead, the start of the Underworld where no mortal man (well, mostly) ever came back from.

And there, on its bank, standing erect in his boat, Charon, the Ferryman.

For an immortal, his appearance was shocking. As gaunt as the oldest of men, his face was haggard and worn, a long straggly beard hiding most everything from his chin down.

Clad in a dark cloak, and carrying a large pole, he cast a sober figure.

Heracles threw up a hand, as if welcoming an old friend.

"Hail, Charon, it has been some time."

"Alive, alive," the old man muttered to himself. "That is all that I see today. Hath the living become so bored that they seek the company of the dead?

"And thee," Charon crooked a bony finger at Heracles, his eyes alighting with a weird hue, "thinkest thou that I hath forgotten thy previous trespass? Thou art still owing the charge of passage!"

Heracles shrugged at the look his companions gave him. "We did have a disagreement over the price of ferrying."

"Disagreement? I was struck down by thee, with mine own pole!"

The demigod fought to hide a grin.

"Are we not kin? Surely family need not pay for passage."

"All must pay the ferryman! Even the Sons of Zeus!"

"We have no time for this," Xanthe reproached the jolly giant. "What is the rate of toll?"

"One gold coin each," Charon said, eyeing them sourly.

Digging into her tunic, the Amazon produced the required amount.

"You said that others have passed this way?"

"Aye, 'twas Zeno, another of Zeus' misbegotten offspring, and his man."

"How long ago?"

"What be time in the Land of the Dead?" the ferryman answered.

Xanthe bit back a comment, instead climbing aboard the boat.

Once all were aboard, Charon pushed off, all the while glaring sullenly at the Scion of Olympus.

As they crossed the black ribbon of water, each was lost in their own thoughts. After a time, they felt a 'thump' as they touched ashore the opposite bank.

"Hold our seats in readiness, we shall have need of them on our return," Heracles quipped.

Grumbling, the ferryman shoved off once his passengers had disembarked.

Before them lay a continuation of the tunnel they had just left.

Once more they followed the path of black stone as it snaked itself through the House of the Dead.

How long they followed it they could not tell, but eventually it came out into a huge room, the biggest space they had seen thus far, save for the river crossing.

And there, in the very center, stood a dais with two large thrones, both of the purest obsidian. One of which was vacant. But the other, oh the other…

There, seated on the throne of his realm, was its master. Hades, dread Lord of the Underworld.

His gray raiment only served to reinforce his pallid features, lending an extra aura of grimness to an already dour figure.

It was to him that fell the task of deciding a man's fate once his life had run its course.

The Elysian Fields, or the pit of Tartarus?

His presence was at once regal and frightening. And all who beheld him did so with a most profound dread. All save one.

"Uncle!" Forgoing all edicts, the demigod mounted the dais.

Xanthe could hear the collective intake of breath from Iochier and Glauce, as if they expected Heracles to be struck down by a bolt of divine lightning.

"How fares the Lord of the Underworld?"

Hades' face was one of utter calm.

"Not well, Heracles. Already, Zeno hath passed this way."

"And you did nothing?" Iochier blurted, clasping his hands to his mouth too late. Yet Hades seemed to take no offense.

"Zeus' edict holds even now, at this late a date. He doth not believe that Zeno will go through with his mad scheme. His affection for his child blinds him to all else.

"I hath been forbidden from impeding him, yet there doth be no compulsion to *aid* him either…"

For the first time, a hint of emotion showed, in the form of a faint smile.

Heracles laughed—perhaps the first that hall had ever known.

"Even now he doth wander through mine domain in search of Tartarus."

"That is good," Xanthe spoke for the first time. "If we can arrive there before him, we can stop him cold."

"Thou shalt hath to do so without mine aid," the god said, once more dour. "As I can not hinder Zeno, neither can I help thee and thine. As such, thou shalt hath to find thy own way, just as he."

"Then let us be on our way. Fear not uncle," Heracles clapped Hades on the back, "your crown is safe."

"May thou meet with success."

With that, the companions made egress to yet another series of tunnels, the beginning of the labyrinth that was the Underworld.

CHAPTER 20

They went not more than a dozen steps before faced with their first decision. Which direction to go?

Before them stood a choice of four ways. Any one of them could lead to Tartarus.

"Logic says that there is safety in numbers," Glauce quoted.

"Yet time is of the essence," Xanthe retorted. "We shall each take a passage."

"What if we should meet with Zeno?"

"Kill him."

Heracles made for one of the openings at random. "Happy hunting!"

Soon each of the party had entered their own tunnel, four adventurers entering into the unknown.

***

Though Heracles had been in the Underworld before, that previous time had been rather quick, and his exploration of the place short. He no more knew where Tartarus was to be found than did anybody else. Yet he did not blanch at the challenge, few were the things that could unnerve the Son of Zeus.

Wicked stepmothers. Gruesome monsters. Rulers of men. All he had handled with aplomb.

Even now, wandering alone in the depths of the Underworld, with the fate of the cosmos hanging in the balance, he did not feel overwhelmed. Such was the confidence and poise of this hero of heroes.

The transition was an abrupt one. One moment he was trekking a rough stone passageway, the next, he was enveloped in an oppressive mist.

He could neither see, nor smell, nor even taste. All his senses were numb, as if the sleeping mind intruded upon wakefulness.

Then, like the mist itself, it passed, and suddenly he was in an open meadow, the expanse of which seemingly went on forever. Where moments before there had been enclosing stone, there was now a cheery sun shining down from a bright blue sky. Not a cloud in sight to mar its brilliance.

The demigod also noticed that he was no longer alone. All about him, frolicking free and easy amongst the wildflowers, were countless men and women.

All happy. All carefree. All dead.

He had found the Elysian Fields, the resting place of the just. A place of contentment and peace.

Heracles reached out to one of the passing shades—the man's forearm was as solid as it might have been in life. In the Underworld, the dead were as lively as the un-dead.

"Are you in need of help?" the man asked, a smile on his face.

"Nay."

Continuing to smile, the shade nodded and went about his way.

The calming influence of the place affected even the Scion of Olympus. This was where all of one's sins were washed away, and only divine acceptance of one's true self and one's place in the universe held ultimate sway. Never had Heracles felt so at ease.

"Heracles!"

Turning at the sound of his name, the demigod saw one that he had known in life, a friend whom had died in a battle long since past.

"Heracles!"

Yet another that he knew. Then another, and another. Many were those who came up to him and wished him well; men, and women too, whom he had known at some point in his life.

Friends, comrades, teachers, all welcomed him. He was glad to receive them, and in doing so, lost all conception of time.

Eventually, he found himself wandering up a gently sloping hill, its grass the green of eternal spring, when the presence of one spirit in particular arrested his attention.

Beautiful she was, true, yet Heracles had seen even more fabulous beauties in his day.

She was also well heeled, her spectral threads bespeaking of refined taste, yet he had seen far more ostentatious bits of finery.

And while the earthy brown hair that flowed below her waist was of a most lustrous sheen, he had seen others with locks even more so.

Yet, the sight of her caused the demigod to stop dead in his tracks.

"Husband," she greeted him, a smile on her lips. "I have never known you to be at a loss for words."

In that moment, Heracles the Hero, Heracles the Scion of Olympus, was replaced by Heracles the man. Heracles the husband.

Shakily, tentatively, he reached out a hand, almost as if he were afraid.

"Have you been a bachelor so long that you can not summon up a greeting for your own wife?" Megara teased, taking his outstretched hand in her own.

His very skin came alive at her touch. Wordlessly, he clutched her close and kissed her.

It was a long time ere they broke their embrace.

"I have forgotten how rough your beard is," she joked.

Heracles said nothing—the tear rolling down his cheek speaking volumes.

Not of sadness, for none could feel such an emotion in this place, but of happiness.

"I have missed you so…"

"I know beloved, I know. I have watched you from here. You have been busy." She paused, concern in her eyes. "And bereaved. I would not see you so. You have always been so full of life, not sorrow. Your heart hangs too heavy."

He stood there, trying, and failing, to find the right words. What does one say to one's dead wife? A wife that is dead due to one's own hand?

Megara tapped her head. "I can read your thoughts, husband. You were never good at hiding them."

"Not from you at least," he conceded. "I have not the words to say what is in my heart…"

"You do yourself a great injustice, husband of mine."

"Nay, it is you that have suffered the injustice. By my own hand no less! Mine!" At his side, his great hands knotted into fists, frustration written clearly upon his face.

Megara shook her head, and placed a hand over his heart.

"It was not of your choosing; to blame yourself for an act that was not your own fault defies logic. It defies common sense." She tilted her head back until she could see into his eyes. "It defies *me*." Her smile was a wry one. "And it is never wise to defy one's wife."

But Heracles' self-contempt would not be so easily assuaged. "Would that I had been struck down instead! To know that I be the instrument of your own destruction!" The demigod ground his fists into his temples, trying to come to terms with his long pent up grief.

"Heracles," Megara slowly brought her husband's hands down to his side. "Hear my words, for our time here is but a short while. You were but a pawn in a larger game. You did not infect your own mind with madness; that was done by another. Would you feel better had it been *I* so afflicted?"

"Nay."

"I thought not. You are the one with broad shoulders, not I. If anyone is strong enough to lift themselves above false guilt, it is you."

She took him by those self same shoulders and playfully shook him.

"I forgive you, husband! Before all the gods, I, Megara, Daughter, Wife, Mother, do absolve you of any and all offenses perpetrated upon myself. I forgive you, I forgive you, I forgive you! It is time for you to forgive yourself," she finished softly.

Her words, combined with this place, did what the Twelve Labors could not: free him of the blame he carried in his breast every moment of every day. To be with his wife again, to enjoy her caustic wit, and her clear-eyed judgment—it was a tonic for what ailed him.

"Ah, I see that I have made a dent in that armor that is your head." Her grin was lopsided. "You have always been not just stronger than a hundred men, but just as stubborn."

Megara's eyes sparkled as she looked beyond her husband.

"It would appear that we have company…"

Heracles turned, following her gaze.

"Father!" the children cried, as they raced over the green sward.

Before he knew it, Heracles' children threw themselves at him, and he good-naturedly fell before the swarm.

This truly was paradise.

"Come now children, let your father up. He has important matters to attend to."

"Nay," he said, "I do not wish to leave. You are here. Our children are here. I would stay."

Megara shook her head wistfully, "Now is the time for you to live, and in so doing, you must see to it that the gods do so as well."

"Bah," he spat, "what care I for the gods? If I am not to be blamed for your presence here, then Hera surely is. Would it not be justice to see her cowed?"

"And what of us?" his wife asked. "Do you seriously think that Zeno would be a just ruler? He would see Hades dethroned as well. Pray tell, which Titan do you think would administer this realm so well as he?

"What is more, Zeno does not strike one as a most forgiving man; and he would have to be most forgiving to allow you—whom have chased him halfway across the world—to go along your merry way. Nay, the heart that burns with revenge cares not for the contentment of others.

"We are at peace here. And there shall come a day when you shall join us. Yet today is not that day." She placed her hands on her hips defiantly.

Though he yearned to gainsay her, Heracles knew that she was right, and that what she spoke of made sense.

"It is no easy thing you ask. For a man to lose his family *twice*..."

"This is not goodbye, rather, farewell until we meet again. Doubt not that our day will come, love. Think of it this way, if you are successful in saving Olympus, the debt they will owe will be immense beyond measure." She grinned, knowing that would appeal to him.

And it did.

With a (not quite so) heavy heart, he got to his feet, and ruffled the hair of his children.

"Come here," Megara said, seductively. "That you may know what is in store for you."

Embracing once more, their lips met for the final time.

As the demigod finally turned to go, Megara stopped him.

"The gods are forbidden from helping you with your task, yet *I* am no god." Mischief to match his own was evident in her eyes as she explained to him the route to take to reach Tartarus.

***

Zeno wondered how long he had been wandering the Underworld. Hours? Days? Weeks even? He simply did not know, for time seemed to have no meaning here.

What was most maddening was at how close he knew himself to be. He was *in* the Underworld, but did not know where anything was. The place was built like a labyrinth. If only he had thought to bring a ball of twine…

***

Xanthe reflected upon the fact that she had not known what to expect once they reached the Underworld. She had supposed that it was a place filled to the brim with the spirits of the dead groping around, lost, not unlike herself.

But there was none of that. Outside of Charon and Hades himself, she had seen naught of the inhabitants of this realm. Presumably they were partitioned off somewhere else other than the endless halls of rock that seemed to riddle the place.

Coming to an intersection, she paused, trying to gauge the best route, when she noticed it: while she had stopped, the echo of footsteps had not.

On guard, she strained her ears to discern where they were coming from. But she need not have bothered.

Steady, relentless, the footfalls sounded closer and closer, their pace keeping time with the beat of Xanthe's heart.

Glauce? Zeno? Something she did not want to know?

"Put aside thy sword, Xanthe of the Amazons."

The Amazon took a step back upon seeing the figure that came from out of the dark recesses.

"Melinoe, Daughter of Hades, Goddess of Ghosts, bids thee welcome."

Statuesque, her gown left little to the imagination. And while she wore a veil, it was not so heavy as to blot out her features. Features as fine and delicate as those of the most beautiful of porcelain dolls. In fact, her appearance was like that of an exquisite mortal woman in every respect, save one. Her coloring.

Her skin was both black as pitch and white as snow, one shade to each side, giving her the appearance of always being half in light and half in shadow.

And she was not alone. She had a retinue of followers, as transparent as their mistress's garments, with as little substance. Men and women both, peasants and royals alike, all clustered about their patron, heedless of the rank they had once held in life.

Her voice was whispery, almost hollow—befitting a daughter of Hades.

"Thou art well met. Though I doubt thou doth see it that way." The hint of a smile (or was it a grimace?) played at her lips. "Few art those whom wish to partake of the Underworld before their time."

Xanthe did not know what to say, lest she say something wrong.

In the interim, Melinoe gazed at her, as though penetrating her very spirit.

"I find thee a puzzle, Xanthe of the Amazons."

The warrior woman at last found her voice. "How so?"

"Why art thou helping us, the gods, in our time of need? We help not even ourselves, yet thou art willing to risk thyself on our behalf."

Xanthe paused before responding. "As you say, you are unable to act on your own behalf, thus someone must."

The Daughter of Hades nodded musingly. "Why?"

"Why," she repeated upon Xanthe's blank stare. "Why should thou care if the gods rule or not? What can it matter to thee? Dost thou think we care for thee? Ask Heracles about the full faith and credit of the gods."

If Xanthe knew not what to say before, she truly was at a loss now.

"We meddle with thy lives, and then expect thee to bow to our wishes and whims. Take thee for instance. Hast thou a family?"

"My sisters."

"Ah, thy fellow Amazons. Yet, no man to call thy own, no children to carry on thy legacy. And why?"

"I am Amazon." That said it all.

"Where is it written that Amazons can not know the value of a man's gentle embrace, or the joy of raising one's own offspring?"

"Goddess Athena—"

"Exactly, Athena," Melinoe interrupted. "the gods tell thee not to. Why should Athena's choice of forsaking such bonds bind thee and thine to the same? What right hath she, hath we, to dictate to thee? We treat thee as pets, yet thou art willing to die for us. Why?"

While confused, Xanthe tried her best to answer.

"If it is as you say, then the ways of the gods are not unlike our own. Though we be a vain and selfish lot, we have value all the same. As such, so too must you. To stand by and allow a thing of value to be destroyed, it does more than wreck the thing itself, it also destroys those whom do nothing to stop it. It is our own selves that are aided in the aiding of others."

"Interesting. Thou would seek to save the selfish for thy own selfish reasons?" The goddess appraised her anew. "I would not think such logic born of an Amazon. There doth be more to thee than meets the eye.

"Indeed, carrying such a proposition one step further, one might say that in so far as the gods art like men, then it stands to reason that men art like gods, in which case to act in the aid of one is to gain the divinity of the other.

"Pray tell, art thou God, or Man, Xanthe?"

"Neither. I am Amazon."

Silence reigned for a moment.

"I hath gained insight from thy words. I find them pleasing. I did wish to know the mettle of which thou wert made. I would see thee aided in thy quest, for truly, I doth not relish the idea of Zeno recreating the cosmos in his image. For all of its perceived gloom, the Underworld doth be mine home.

"As a goddess, I doth be forbidden by Zeus' edict to give thee direct aid. However," she turned to her ghostly followers, "they doth not be gods, merely ghosts. As such, they art under no such prohibition." And now, for the first time, the goddess openly smiled.

The next few minutes were to be like no conversation Xanthe had ever had before.

***

Iochier had begun to think that splitting up had not been such a good idea. Sure, any one of them might stumble upon Zeno, but the odds were even better that any one of them might get lost in these catacombs. Like he was now.

The prevailing gloom of the Underworld had a tendency to bring to light all of one's secret fears. The one uppermost on his mind at the moment being trapped here. The more he thought about it, the more likely it seemed.

However, Iochier's growing fears were cut off suddenly when he found himself entering what could only be described as a large banquet hall.

In the center stood a long table, plied high with all manner of scrumptious looking food, the smell of which caused the would-be warrior's stomach to rumble. And all around the table were finely wrought chairs, carved from the living rock.

And there, occupying one of the chairs, sat a man.

"Greetings," the man said, throwing up a hand. "I would stand, yet alas, I can not do so."

Curious, Iochier came closer, and upon doing so, could plainly see why the man could not in fact stand: from the legs down he was encased in stone.

"Yes," the other said, "gaze upon the folly of Man. Punishment for trifling with the gods."

Something about all of this rang a bell...

"You are—"

"Pirithous, formally King of Lapithus, now permanent guest of Hades."

Pirithous! Iochier's eyes nearly burst from their sockets. If one were to speak of men of action, Pirithous was perhaps the prototype! He had dared to come to the Underworld to abscond with a bride—one that already belonged to Hades!

As might be imagined, Hades had been none too fond of the idea. Thus, when he had gotten wind of the plot, he tricked Pirithous by offering the king hospitality, a feast. And when Pirithous sat down to it, Hades had him trapped in the very chair upon which he now sat.

A chair upon which he was to sit for all eternity, as a punishment.

"I hope you have not come here to take away someone. I can tell you from experience that it is not worth it."

"N-nay. I am in search of Tartarus."

The king raised an eyebrow. "What manner of sin could you have committed that has led you to seek out Tartarus, rather than trying to avoid it, like any sensible man?"

"It is nothing such as that. I am pursuing one who seeks it."

Pensively, Pirithous rubbed his chin. "If it is Tartarus you seek, you are quite a bit out of your way."

Iochier sighed. He was afraid of that.

"However, I could tell you how to find it."

Hope springs eternal.

"Speak man, speak! The cosmos hangs in the balance!"

"First, I would ask a boon."

"Such as?"

"Conversation. It is not often that I have visitors. Sit and pass the time with me and I will tell you what you wish to know."

"There is no time," Iochier exclaimed, trying to impress upon the other his urgency. "Every minute I spend here is another minute that Zeno is closer to his goal."

"Which would be?"

"The overthrow of the gods!"

"Interesting. I would hear more of this." Pirithous put his hands behind his head, obscenely at ease for a man trapped in stone.

Hurriedly, Iochier informed the former king of Zeno and his plan to free the Titans and to take over Mount Olympus, and how he, Iochier, was part of a group of champions entrusted with seeing that such did not happen.

By the end of it, Pirithous gave him a long, searching, look.

"You do not appear the warrior type, Iochier," the king stated. "What is more, upon further review, why should I wish to help the gods—it is one of their number by whom I be trapped! Perhaps a new 'manager' of the Underworld would look more favorably upon my plight."

Iochier could not believe what he was hearing.

"What sort of king are you? That you would allow your people to suffer, as most assuredly they must in any war of the gods! You would place your own well being above that of your subjects? Any king who would do so is not deserving of the crown upon their head!"

"Who are you to lecture? What laurels have you won, what deeds have you accomplished? You are but a boy. My name is one that rings to this day. Yours is unfamiliar to any beyond your own family."

Iochier flushed at the words. But true or no, they did not sway his opinion.

"Who I am is of little consequence. What matters is that I know right from wrong, which appears to be more than you. If I am as lowly as you say, and *I* know the right thing to do, what does that say about *you*?"

Pirithous' look was both long, and appraising.

"You would try and find Tartarus whether I tell you or no, is that not true?"

"Yes," the other huffed.

"There is courage in that. And courage is a rare enough quality amongst men. It should be nurtured and rewarded."

Another pause.

"I shall tell you the way to Tartarus, youngling. Though I do not find it to my own advantage, there is truth in all that you have said. My actions aside, I do care about those who were once my subjects, and would not be gladdened to have hastened their demise.

"Yet, of more import still, that you, who are woefully unprepared for this task, would still try—I find that impressive. I think perhaps that there be something princely of you."

So it was that Pirithous told the young warrior what he wished to know.

***

Glauce had begun to think that this whole splitting up idea had been a mistake. The more she wandered around alone in the Underworld, the more she missed her companions.

She found herself going over in her mind the number of people whom had visited this place and returned to tell about it. It was a depressingly short list.

She had just turned a corner when she was suddenly thrust into a thick mist. Instinctively, she stepped back—and was once more in the tunnel.

Curious, she stepped forward again, and again was immersed in a fog. Back, forward and back again, the rhapsode determined that this must be an immortal veil of some kind. Perhaps she had found Tartarus?

With a mixture of excitement and trepidation, she pushed on, even as the gloom enveloped her.

Unable to see even the hand in front of her face, she groped around blindly, thrusting her staff out in front of her.

Soon, the fog dissipated, and Glauce was confronted with a broad vista. Gone were the dark, dreary tunnels of the Underworld. In their place was a slightly less dreary landscape.

The sky overhead was gray and overcast with clouds threatening to rain.

Even the grassy plain was of a dull, lifeless hue. Not exactly what she pictured Tartarus to be like.

"The Gray Lands," a voice said behind her.

Turning, Glauce saw a well-dressed man with a lyre.

"You look confused," the man said. "It is natural. Most are upon entry here. This is where one goes when one has not been particularly evil, yet neither has one been particularly good. It is a gray area of morality, thus the name of the place.

"Speaking of names, mine is Linus. I would welcome you here, however…" He gestured at the featureless surroundings and shrugged.

Glauce's eyes widened as recognition set in.

"Are you the same Linus who—"

"Is known the world over? Yes."

He was nothing if not immodest. But Glauce could not rightly hold that against him. In his day, he was renowned, arguably the greatest rhapsode of the age. His pupils were legion. Accounting among their number everyone from philosophers to kings to even demigods.

To the young woman, he represented the heights of her profession.

"I see that you are a rhapsode, just as myself. Doubtlessly not as talented, yet it speaks well of you. This dreary realm needs such as us, I know just the place for you…"

Glauce had to force herself not to go with him; such was the force of the man's personality.

"I am flattered, however, I fear you are mistaken. I be not dead, yet rather a visitor, not a resident."

Linus halted, looking at her anew.

"Alive, you say? What fool you must be to come to the Underworld. What possible reason could compel the living to consort with the dead?"

"A quest, tasked by the gods. I must find Tartarus."

"The gods you say? To what purpose could the gods have to send a rhapsode into the depths of Hades' lair? Let alone a mere girl."

'Mere girl'? Glauce let it pass.

"It is the gods themselves that I aid. It is imperative that I reach Tartarus posthaste. Can you help?"

Linus appeared to either have not heard, or not care.

"Of what service could a rhapsode be to the gods?"

Glauce's admiration for the man was rapidly becoming tinged with annoyance.

"It is my strong right arm more than my voice that Athena has called upon."

"Arms? Quests?" Linus snorted. "A good rhapsode tells of great deeds, he does not become a participant in them! Otherwise, there can be no impartiality, no honest brokering of the facts.

"Leave the gods to their own devices, child," he commiserated. "Wars should be waged by warriors, not wordsmiths."

Glauce was too flabbergasted to respond. Linus took her silence as license to continue.

"It is the Muses that should be your patrons, not Athena. Though wise, what does she know of the ways of the rhapsode? Our trade is stories, not swords."

As Linus continued his harangue, Glauce feared that she was to gain no help from this quarter. As such, she needed to find someone who *would* help her, and fast.

"I beg pardon," she interrupted. "Though I can respect your opinions, as anyone of our profession must, large events are in motion, and my presence is required. If you will not help—"

"Large events, you say?" Linus broke in. "What sort of 'large events'?"

Approaching the point of exasperation, Glauce filled Linus in as quickly as possible as to the extent of the dire circumstances at hand.

"By the gods," the other breathed, "do you know what you are doing?"

Frustrated, she was about to retort when he went on.

"You are bearing witness to the most significant event in the history of the world since the Titanomachy! To be the chronicler of such a thing…" His eyes took on a glossy sheen. "It is an opportunity that comes but once every thousand generations! Participation or no, a rhapsode *must* be there!"

Glauce had no time to register her surprise as Linus launched into excruciating detail the way to Tartarus.

CHAPTER 21

In the end, it was Trepat who found the way. Losing sight of his master as he turned a bend, he had wandered down a different tunnel.

Noticing his servant gone, Zeno had turned back, annoyed. But all thoughts of recriminations were driven from his mind when saw what Trepat was looking at.

While the entrance had been barely wide enough for one man, the chamber itself could only be described as titanic. And against its back wall was a metal portcullis that stretched up into the shadows. More massive than even the gates guarding the entrance of the Underworld itself.

What was more, Zeno could feel himself growing warm, a palpable heat, increasing with every moment. It was with fascination that Zeno noted that he had begun to sweat. So had Trepat, though his was a cold one.

He could hear, faintly at first, as though from a great distance, but increasingly closer, a sound. Something between a howl and a yell.

Like that of the damned.

The godling closed his eyes, allowing the thrill of the moment to wash over him. Neither mortals nor immortals had been able to deny him. This, this was what he had been born for.

All that stood between him and his destiny was a simple winch, with which to raise the portcullis and his reign.

"Trepat, you may have the honors."

Less than thrilled, Trepat put his shoulder to the winch and pushed, straining to raise the giant gate.

***

It was taking longer than it should.

"Put your back into it!" Zeno roared.

The perspiration dripped from Trepat as he muscled the gate upwards.

"Had we but wine, Trepat!" Zeno mused, wistfully. "This is a moment that demands a toast. To my victory! My ascendancy! My transmogrification! My—"

"End."

Head swiveling wildly, Zeno saw emerge from the shadows one whom he had thought slain. Then again, perhaps she was, this was the Underworld after all.

"Be you spirit or flesh, know that you can not alter what the Fates have decreed!"

Xanthe was not impressed. In truth, she was not even listening to Zeno's ranting. Instead, she was focused on stopping him here, now, at all costs. Up to, and including, her own life.

After all, she was already in the Underworld.

Drawing her sword, she advanced, the look on her face doing her talking for her.

But Zeno was not to be cowed; he was too close, too close to achieving everything that he wanted. Such was his frenzy that he did not even bother to draw his own blade.

"Do you not feel it?" he queried, a smile playing at his lips.

Even as he spoke, Xanthe could feel a trembling resonating through the floor. It was faint at first, but with every stride it increased, like the slow building of an earthquake.

"Behold! A new age dawns! I have an entire *army* at my beck and call, an army of the *dead*! Hear them, they come to proclaim their allegiance to their new master!"

Xanthe could feel the sweat trickling down the back of her neck, and it had nothing to do with the oppressive heat.

An army of the dead. All the spirits of all the people who had ever been cast into the pit of Tartarus, unleashed upon an unsuspecting world. And at the back of *them*, the Titans.

Xanthe struggled as horror clutched at her heart. Not even her fierce Amazonian determination could steel her against the enormity that she was now face to face with. The howling hordes of the undead, ripe for revenge against a living world that mocked them by the very act of being alive.

Time itself seemed to slow, the unreality of the situation playing havoc with her senses. Everything was so clear.

Zeno, cut in a fine relief, his head thrown back in maniacal laughter.

The gate, the size of which was beyond scope, every fraction of movement sealing the fate of both Man and Gods.

The windlass, moving the chain, link by agonizing link, all cumulating towards—

Then it hit her: without that windlass and chain, the portcullis would come crashing down. And with it, all of Zeno's mad hopes.

Like a white-hot iron, fear was replaced by hope. And the sheer radiance of it burned away the fog of defeat that had threatened to swallow her whole.

It was some moments before Zeno noted her actions, and some moments more before realization dawned on him.

It was his turn to feel horror as he gleaned what Xanthe had in mind, and what it meant for all of his well laid plans.

Loosening his own sword, he scrambled across the shifting floor to head the Amazon off.

Such was the intensity of their focus on one another, that none noticed the new arrivals.

Through the partially open gate they streamed, a shambling horde, twisted mockeries of what had once been living men (and women). Grotesque parodies, half mad with pain, and showing fully the signs of damnation upon their bodies.

Bloated, blotchy, their features were macabre masks, as though made from melted wax. Their garments rent, their hands bloodied, their eyes devoid of any sense of reason; only an animal fierceness remained, a hunger that they had not slaked while alive.

Screaming incoherently, Zeno sliced at Xanthe, trying to cut her down, but the Amazon caught the attack on her blade and swept it aside. And though off balance, she used it to her advantage, allowing herself to sink to the floor a split second before Zeno's sword passed back over her head.

Like a top, she spun around, her whirling legs causing the demigod to leap back, thus allowing her to regain her feet.

A strike to the right, blocked. To the left, blocked. Up, down, Zeno could not seem to get through her defenses as she showed what an Amazon upbringing brought to the table.

Parry, block, stab, cut; a choreographer could not have drafted a better looking dance.

Xanthe sidestepped an attack, but before she could capitalize, Zeno's elbow fouled her swing in passing.

Turning with the speed of a cobra, the godling sought to gut the Amazon, who avoided the cut only by virtue of her own lightning like reflexes.

Snapping her head forward, she slammed it into Zeno's face, the impact of which caused both of them to stumble back.

The blond battler tried to clear her head when she felt a hand at her shoulder. Quickly turning, she found herself face to face with a horror.

The face (if it could be called that) was a ruinous mass of mangled discolored flesh, revealing in places pale bone. And in it there was one roving orb looking back at her with a fiery light, the other socket empty of anything.

Zeno forgotten for the moment, Xanthe's revulsion at the sight that greeted her caused her to jerk violently, wrenching herself from the creature's grasp. Free, she thrust her sword through the walking corpse's vitals. Or at least, what had once been its vitals. As it was, the blade had no effect.

Grinning, the fiend reached out to grab her again. Fear lending speed to her limbs, she cut at the thing as though it were a blade of grass, cleaving it to the spine, and coming out the other side.

The zombie collapsed to the floor, now harmless as a detached torso and legs.

But he was not alone. Doomed spirits poured forth from the partially raised gate as water from a dam, fighting each other for the chance to escape.

"Behold!" crowed Zeno. "My day has come! Witness the beginning of a new reign, Amazon! Know that no one can stay my hand now!"

"It is a good thing that we are not 'one', save rather, many!"

The voice raised the Amazon's spirits even as it dashed Zeno's.

With great sweeping arcs of his war club, Heracles cleared waves of the shambling miscreants aside like so many ten pins.

And in his wake, Glauce and Iochier too threw themselves against the vast undead hordes.

They strode boldly to abate the tide of death that threatened to sweep over them all.

The sight gave new vigor to Xanthe. Even if they all fell this day, to have lived to see such an assemblage of courage made it worthwhile.

"It will avail you not!" Zeno screamed. "Do you not hear? They have come!"

The rumbling that had been getting louder had also been getting *closer*.

The Titans! They were coming! And from the sound of things, would not be long in doing so! This had to end now.

No words. No banter. No proclamations. Xanthe launched her attack without ado, bent upon one thing: Zeno's head on a pike.

It was an onslaught born of fury and fear.

Almost faster than the human eye could follow, the sound of their blades meeting rang out like the keening of a bell. The slightest mistake, the merest hesitancy, and it would be the end.

The heat, the undead, the coming of the Titans, Xanthe blocked it all out as she pushed Zeno back, step by step. Her teeth clenched, her arm aching with each stroke of the sword given and received, she fought through it all, determined to achieve her goal.

For Zeno's part, madness lent strength to what would otherwise have been a spent figure. He would not be denied, not now!

And all the while, the portcullis crept slowly upwards, more and more of the undead streaming out.

Fortunately, they paid scant attention to Xanthe. Unfortunately, that was due to all of their attention being focused on her companions.

Companions who were at the moment in great peril.

Iochier, Glauce, and Heracles had been pushed back to back to back by the great tide of rotting flesh. Though not incredibly formidable by themselves, their sheer numbers proved to be a threat to even Heracles himself, like a bear before the march of ants.

"It would seem," Glauce said, ducking the would be embrace of one of the sub-creatures, instead sinking her staff deep into his mid section before bringing it up under his chin, clearing him out of the way, "that dead men *can* tell tales. Or at least play a part in their creation."

But no amount of asides could hide the dread that hung unspoken about them. They were going to meet their end here. And there was naught they could do about it.

And while they fought for their lives, their companion fought for something else. For Xanthe, it was not just about them, or even the gods, but something larger, more nebulous. It was about who she was, *what* she was. And what she was, was an Amazon. And if that was worth anything, anything at all, then it had to be worth fighting for. Otherwise it was all a lie, a profound joke to which she was the punch line.

And Xanthe was not known for her sense of humor.

Her slice was blocked, but she had anticipated that. Using her free hand, she grasped Zeno's, suddenly rendering his sword immobile.

And then, before he could react, she kicked him in the nether regions (the irony was not lost on either of them).

In that split second, Xanthe freed her arms, and then, with a speed born of desperation, she plunged her sword into Zeno's guts.

Or at least, she tried to. Instead of meeting the fleshy resistance she had expected, the blade simply slid into him, as though he were made of clay, leaving him none the worse for the wear.

Xanthe's disorientation was matched only by Zeno's own. It would have been comical were it not so macabre.

And then he laughed, a high, disturbing laugh.

"What fools are we? The fruit! The Fruit of Immortality! As long as its effects last, no harm can befall us!"

The fight forgotten for the moment, the godling gave vent to his amusement. Xanthe, she had a different reaction: she punched Zeno in the face.

A punch followed by a roundhouse to the head, followed by a kick to the ribs, followed by a chop to the throat.

Perhaps he could not be killed, but he could feel pain.

As Zeno gagged, the Amazon brought a knee up, the sound it made as it connected with his chin causing even the undead to wince.

In that short order, Zeno, the would-be master of the cosmos, slumped down to the now unstable stone floor.

As if on the swaying deck of a ship, Xanthe walked over to where Trepat was still straining against the windlass and tapped him on the shoulder.

His hands fairly flew off of the wheel as he ran, causing the portcullis to come crashing down, catching not a few of the undead in the process.

And not a moment too soon, for the thundering reached its crescendo. The Titans had arrived. A moment late and a dinar short.

But while the worst had been averted, there was still the matter of the hordes of undead on the loose.

Almost as soon as she had thought it, Xanthe felt a hand at her own shoulder. Startled, she found it to be Hades.

"If I may…"

At the sight of the Lord of the Underworld, the undead stopped in their tracks, as though frozen in fear. As well they were.

With the wave of a hand, the god sent about a whirlwind that swept through the chamber, scooping up all of those whom had attempted to flee their punishment. Like leaves before the wild hurricane fly, they cast about, a great wail of disappointment emanating from them.

"The windlass, if thou wilt," the god asked.

Xanthe hesitated. The Titans were at the very gate itself, their massive frames could just be glimpsed beyond the shadowy portal. If the portcullis were to be raised, what would stop them from coming through? Though a god, even Hades alone would not trouble their number.

"The Titans—"

"Shalt be no trouble."

Surprised for a second time, Xanthe saw none other than Athena in all of her regal glory. Seeming all the more out of place in this, the very pits of the Underworld.

The goddess strode over to where Zeno slumped on the floor, unconscious. Contemptuously, she grabbed the quiver from his back that contained Zeus' stolen Thunderbolts.

"I think Father shalt not object to mine having use of one of his Thunderbolts in this situation," she said, smiling. "What say thee, Heracles?"

The demigod's laugher was the only response.

Situating herself in front of the gate, armed with the heavenly missiles, she stood silently, grimly daring those on the other side to do something as Xanthe slowly raised the portcullis.

She need not have bothered. Angry, wrathful, they yet stood their ground, impotent before the display of godly might.

The task completed, Xanthe once again lowered the gate.

"Thou did well," the Goddess of Wisdom said, praising the heroes. "Thou hath accomplished a feat denied even the gods themselves. There doth be a lesson in that."

"Pray tell Hera that the next time you see her!" Heracles said pointedly.

Athena allowed herself a small smile.

"I doth be proud of all of thee." The goddess looked upon the warrior with kindly eyes. "Pray tell Amazon, what hath thou learned?"

Xanthe was not sure how to respond, she was a raging cauldron of conflicting emotions. So many of her preconceived notions had been challenged during this venture. Of men, of her sisters, of even the gods themselves.

Her response was slow, almost halting.

"I did think that men and gods were different in all the important ways, and the same only in the most superficial. Yet, it seems," her voice faltered a moment before finding the strength to go on. "It seems as though it is the differences that are superficial, that it is the ways in which Man and God are the same that truly matter.

"Like us, you know fear, and avarice. In tasting the fruits of immortality, I have not gained any new insight, nor anything at all which I did not have before; I am still me, only more. If this be true for me, then it seems that it would be true for you and yours, great lady."

Athena's smile widened.

"Thou *hast* learned much from this. And fear not, dear Xanthe. There doth be no offense in the words thou hast said, though some of mine order may not feel the same."

Heracles snorted.

"In fact, thy words please me, for they show wisdom. And what more could please the Goddess of Wisdom than the finding of it in her children?"

Her words were like a soothing balm to Xanthe's still excited state. Though she knew what she said to be true, still there had been the lingering doubt that they were blasphemous.

"What is to be done with him?" the blond battler asked, gesturing to Zeno.

"Now that brother Zeus' edict no longer applies, I doth hath a place for him," Hades replied, the smile on his face eliciting only dread from those who saw it. "Art thou acquainted with the fate of Sisyphus…?"

"What of the other one, the servant?" Iochier suddenly remembered.

"The Underworld doth be quite a difficult place to navigate unless one knows where one is going. I hath no fear that he shalt find his own place in my dominion."

And with that, the God of the Underworld clapped a hand on Zeno's shoulder and in a flash of light disappeared, leaving only Athena and the companions.

It was left to Iochier to voice the obvious question, "Now what?"

The goddess smiled. "Thou art free to go as thou please. I shalt transport thee to where ever it is that thou doth wish."

"For myself," Heracles proclaimed, "I have heard tell of a monster in Crete, half man and half bull, that the locals must placate with the sacrifice of maidens. And even if there be no monster, at least there is the hope of maidens!

"What say you, friend Iochier? I could use a man such as you at my side. Wine, women, and the promise of adventure, what more could a man, or a demigod, ask for?"

Iochier jumped at the chance.

Heracles held out his hand to Xanthe, by way of parting.

"You are a fine ambassador of your people, and the Son of Zeus is proud to have traveled with you.

And prouder still to call you friend—if you will permit it."

Xanthe clasped his forearm, her grin matching the demigod's own. "You are permitted."

The demigod turned to Glauce. "And goodbye to you, little one. You now have a tale worth telling. It is not many whom can claim to have *one* god in their debt, let alone all of them!"

Slapping an arm around Iochier's shoulders, the Scion of Olympus started walking away.

"Have you ever heard of the time I slew the Stymphalian Birds…?"

And then, in a swirl of light, the two were gone.

"And what of thee, Xanthe of the Amazons?" Athena asked, her attention on the remaining women.

"I should like to go home to see my queen. There is much that I would discuss with her."

Athena nodded knowingly. "And of thee?" she asked of Glauce.

The rhapsode looked at Xanthe before responding.

"I should like to visit my sisters once more. After all, they are my family."

"Well said."

Athena looked long and searchingly at the two of them, her face thoughtful.

"The world hast not heard the last of thee. Of this I doth be sure."

The two women looked at one another. If this was just the beginning, what else was in store?

THE END